# Buckeye Lake

# Summer 1949

## Take Care of Paula for me

### Patte Burgoon

12-29-'14

To My Star I love

Sharon,
Love, Patte

Photos used with permission of The Greater Buckeye Lake
Historical Society Museum

Author's photo by Sharon Deevey

*That Summer*
Cover art by Jacob Erb, Copyright©2014 Jacob Erb

PUBLISHED BY
THE EDUCATIONAL PUBLISHER INC.
BIBLIO PUBLISHING
BIBLIOPUBLISHING.COM

ISBN-PRINT: 978-1-62249-228-2
ISBN-eBOOK: 978-1-62249-229-9

## Dedication

To my "magnificent seven": Lisa, Paul (dec.) Karl, John, Reid, Kristin and Gina who provided me with the necessities through good health and poor. You and the book have given me reason to put one foot in front of the other one on many dark days. To your mates: Richard, Marji, and Kevin who make you happy, I couldn't love you more. I dedicate my words to you all in thanks.
…also to the United Hearts of the World for PEACE.

## Remembering

**Nancy Zimmer Helpman**

**Dick Leindecker**

**Chance (Sonny) Brockway**

**Jim Roelle**

**Otho Zimmer, Sr.**

**Otho (Sonny) Zimmer, Jr.**

# TABLE OF CONTENTS

## Acknowledgements

My gratitude has no boundaries. It did indeed take a village or two for me to be able to complete this book. Six years of life's interruptions without so much as a '...by your leave, ...' I have reentered my task of completion again and again. When I read about other authors and how they discipline their lives, treating writing as a job ... I can't do that. I am a participator in life. Therefore, I took time out for surgeries, funerals, celebrations and a weekend here and there to be with my family (my *raison d'etre*).

So many of you have helped in more than one way. I struggled with ways to give you all space on a billboard. Some would be mentioned once and some as many as ten times. You see my dilemma? I have concluded that I will mention your name once and with deep affection. Know that you are appreciated beyond time and space for everything you did, be it large or small, that helped me in my first effort to produce a coming of age novel. I am acutely aware of every little thing you did for me be it advice, a memory, a dinner, a boat ride around the lake, editing, suggestions for clarity, acknowledgement for sensitivities of characters, photos, and rescues from the printed word such as a day trip here and there. Many of you have honored my need for non-interruptions and welcomed me back with open arms when I surfaced.

The correct word in just the right place makes all the difference. Your technology skills have me in awe. I even have to thank Mavis Beacon for her help. I regret that some of my cheerleaders were called home before I had my manuscript ready. They are with me on the other side of the vale. I suspect they even helped a time or two. The list of names I owe so much gratitude is not in any particular order. Please know that I love you and thank you for your assistance when I needed you most: J-Me Braig, Sonny

Roelle, Chance Brockway (dec.), Dick Leindecker (dec.), the entire Jim Bartoe family (Nick and Pinkie too), Lias Erb, Karl Oberer, John Eric Oberer, Reid Oberer, Kristin Grace, Gina Ryan, Barb and Julie Callahan, Dick Helpman, Bob Farrington, "my friend" Donna Pangalangan, JoE and Gordon Miller, John and Joan Forkin, Jane Wimberly, Terri Pimental, Annie Sullivan, Margi Williams, Dennis Rogers, Pam Mormile, Susi Miller, Nasr Misak, Dolly Argue, Joe Sardella, Nancy Hawk, Michael Brooks, Tom Musick, Sheila Moody, Jan Teter, Norm Brown, Chuck Peterman, Paula Pare, Frances Rowe, Sarah and Jay Watson. Take a breath. The older you get the more people there are to thank.

To continue …Pamela Hamilton, Margo Bebinger, Beth Swan, Jacob Erb, Rick and Michael Marchant, Ken Ryan, Sharon Deevey, Jeannetta Holliman, Carol Rosebrough, Ruthmary Mangan, Kym Hackenberger, Linda Fuches and the Gillie Writers Group. Thank you to Jeanne Marlowe and the IWWG discussion Group.

A very special "thank you" to Bob Sims, President of Biblio Publishing for his guidance, gentle critiquing and special treatment of people and photos.

I would be remiss not to mention Regina Hanneman and Mary Lou Vishey for convincing me to give Columbus a chance and even making it possible to do so. … and then there is Romeo, my impatient cat.

With love, Patte

# Chapter I
## Trip Down Memory Lane

Paula Bradley returns to Columbus, Ohio after a 45 year hiatus. She is driven to retrace her steps to see if the amusement park at Buckeye Lake, Ohio is still intact. It's now spring, 1994. Why is she so shocked to find that nothing is the same? It was once called 'The Playground of Ohio.'

She recognizes only the fountain that graced the park entrance in 1949. Heading on to Picnic Point she is disappointed by the removal of weeping willow trees, which stood at either end of the foot bridge connecting the park area to Picnic Point. The Community Church and the shelter house are gone. A whole chapter of her life ... wiped out.

Sitting at one of the new picnic benches eating her peanut butter sandwich she catches herself humming an old Appalachian hymn that a few of her friends sang back then.

"*Hmm hmmm . . . a mountain railroad.* Hmm hmmm *engineer that's brave . . .*" She remembers the tune but some of the words aren't coming. She watches wakes made by a couple of speed boats. Someone launches a boat from winter storage using the new ramp. Paula is pleased to see a couple of portable toilets installed. The brisk wind on the point nudges Paula to return to her car. *"Hmm hmmm curves that fill the tunnel hmm hmmm. ... "*

Walking the shoreline on her way back to the footbridge Paula notices something snagged on a stick: protruding from the steep bank at the water's edge Paula squints then recognizes it to be a spent condom. The summer of 1949 floods her memory… her being. It forces her back through time, to relive her initiation into a different reality. One that replaced her dreams and expectations when she thought she knew a whole lot concerning what life was all about. If she could just get to the picnic bench, she could regain her balance.

* * *

Buckeye Lake is a special place for Paula Bradley. The water's not blue. There's no tide. The floating islands are less than pleasant to touch when you slip out of the boat for a dip on a moonlit night. There isn't much sand. Everything a teenage girl could want is here in 1949: jobs, fun things to do, a place to hang out, bowling lanes, a swimming pool, skating rink and plenty of boys.

# CHAPTER II
## THE INVITATION

Father Porter makes the sign of the cross in Paula's direction in the confessional. "Say three Our Fathers, three Hail Mary's and make a good Act of Contrition." After murmuring absolution in Latin, he slides the hatched speakeasy door to the closed position. Paula slips out of the confessional and goes to the side altar to say her penance. The larger than life statue of the Blessed Mother is guarded by the flicker of the vigil lights and shrouded with the aroma of incense.

Paula quietly exits St. Francis church where she's gone to mass and attended school under the tutelage of the Dominican sisterhood for eight years. She is now a freshman at St. Mary of the Springs Academy under their continued guidance. It's a beautiful March day. Paula feels fresh and clean after going to confession. She notices opened daffodils and crocuses, and decides to walk home rather than take the bus. She needs time to process the changes about to take place in her life.

\* \* \*

Two blocks into her walk she sees Millie Chester, her next door neighbor and friend since third grade "Millie, are you lost?" Paula calls,

"Oh! Hi Paula! I'm not lost. I've been working on a class project with a school friend. I'm dead tired and starving. Where have you been?" Millie quizzes.

"I went to confession and decided to walk home. I haven't seen you in over a week and I have some great news to tell you." Paula continues as she changes shoulders for her purse so she can link her arm through Millie's.

"I know. I've been so busy with homework, Easter clothes shopping and all. What's going on? How are the hillbillies working out?" Millie's family calls everyone south of Circleville "hillbillies."

Paula fills her in. "Mother moved us to the basement after some minor adjustments to the space. The Martin family from Portsmouth is renting our house temporarily while my dad and sister, Jeniece, are living in Junction City with my grandparents. Their health is not good, you know."

With a surprised look Millie says, "No! I didn't know."

Paula adds, "I've become sort of friends with Martin's son, George. I told him my rabbit is going to have babies, but I don't know when. He says he'll take a look at her for me. He might be able to tell me how far along she is because he used to keep rabbits in Portsmouth. He pulls 'Mopsie' out of her pen by her ears. I had a hissy fit because I hate it when people pick rabbits up by the ears instead of by the napes of their necks like you'd lift a cat. Anyway, he pets her and gives her a good feel. He busts out laughing. I couldn't get him to stop. He finally settles down long enough to give me the news."

"What's so funny?" Millie asks.

"George says in his best Appalachian Portsmouth accent, 'Your Mopsie ain't gonna have no babies very soon.' I ask, "How do you know?" He blurts out "Cause Mopsies got balls." He stretches out 'balls' for at least three musical counts."

Millie and Paula laugh. Not only is the message a surprise but the way George says 'balls' is priceless.

Adding to their fit of laughter, Millie says "The other day I heard him call your dog a 'Cockerel Spaniard.'"

"You know," Paula reminds Millie, "I was going to give your little brothers a bunny each for Easter. So much for those plans! All I can do now is give Mopsie to your mother to cook for Easter dinner."

"No way!" Millie shrieks.

After more squealing and laughing, Millie interjects some news of her own. "Mother and dad decided to rent out the attic room since my grandma died and we kids don't use it for a playroom anymore."

"Yes. Well, we're growing up, aren't we?" Paula looks at Millie for agreement. "Much as we have to fight to get our parents to acknowledge the fact ... Remember my mentioning to you about my new friend at school, Annie Harper? She and I play duets together on the piano."

"Yes. What about her?" Millie asks as they turn left on Third Avenue.

Paula continues to explain, "Her family lives with her grandmother who owns the Parkview Hotel, around the corner from White Cross Hospital on Park St."

"I can't picture a hotel there." Millie says with a grimace.

Paula continues, "Next time you are on your way to Central High and the bus is going down Goodale St., look for a red brick building on the corner of Park and Goodale. It overlooks Goodale Park. Thus, 'Parkview Hotel.'"

Millie smiles, "Makes sense! So now I know 'who' and 'where.' So, what's the 'what'?"

`"Two nights ago my mother gets a phone call from Annie's dad. He says how pleased he is that Annie and I have become such good friends and how Annie didn't know anyone when we started school in September. He and mother make small talk for a while. Then he says he's been separated from his wife for some time and finally decides to get a divorce. Annie never told me about a divorce ..." No sooner did she say that, Paula has an 'ah-ha' moment. "... maybe Annie didn't know."

Millie sympathizes, "That's so sad. I don't know anybody personally who's gotten a divorce ... just in the movies."

As they pass Hoggets' drugstore, Paula offers, "Want a drumstick? You said you were starving and I've got some change."

"Sure! Sounds good. . . . That won't ruin my dinner. Back to Annie's dad. He didn't call just to tell your mother he's getting a divorce, did he? … Did he want to take her out for a beer?" Millie senses she doesn't have enough details yet.

"No, silly!" Paula fills in, "He wants her to know that every year before Easter he moves his family from the Parkview Hotel to Buckeye Lake, Ohio."

Millie interrupts, "Buckeye Lake! Can't wait! My family is renting a cottage in Millersport the last two weeks in July. You can join us for a few days like you did four or five summers ago."

"Just wait!" Paula shushes her. "He told Mother he heard my folks are living apart right now, grandparents being old, sick and all. Mother told him that Dad had already enrolled Jeniece in second grade in Junction City. So ... Mr. Harper asked mother if she'd consider letting me spend the summer at Buckeye Lake. He says Annie and I will be good for each other and that his eight-year-old son, Rusty, will be with him most of the time."

Millie draws in a deep breath and shoves Paula on the arm. "Are you kidding?"

"Nope! He's renting a furnished house and says he'll pay me to work for him in the Park- Buckeye Lake, 'Playground of Ohio.' Can you believe it?"

"All summer?" Millie shakes her head in disbelief,

"Yep! All summer. You know I was fighting against having to move to Junction City," Paula reminds Millie.

Millie reminds Paula back, "You always loved Junction City. Don't you miss your dad and little sister?"

"Yes … but I'm 14 now. I have other interests besides swimming in the 'crick,' picking wild berries, and walking to the farm across the road to see if my farm friend can play. And she never can. "That was 'kid stuff' ago."

"So, you want to go?" - Millie seeks affirmation. - "Thanks for the drumstick."

"Are you kidding? I have been dancing a jig ever since I heard about it. Mother talks to Dad that very night. He agrees it's a good plan. He doesn't want a sullen teenager on his hands in 'small farm town,' U.S.A. Dad said he'd rent a little house in town so that the three of them, mother, dad and Jeniece, can have some privacy as a family again. He can go out to the farm daily to check on Grandpaw and Maw Emmy. He said Buckeye Lake is close enough that if I get too homesick or unhappy for any reason, he can rescue me. Of course, he has to add '. . . as long as Mr. Harper takes care of Paula.' Everybody wants somebody else to take care of Paula." She rolls her eyes and shrugs.

* * *

Millie declares, "That is the 'what' if I ever heard it. Do you worry about being on your own, kind of? How will you handle that?"

Paula kicks a rock as if it were a football. "I've given it a lot of thought. As far as Mr. Harper's being my substitute parent for the summer, I don't know, Millie. I figure it this way. Remember all the talks you and I have had about religion and confession and all? I figure if I budget my sins like I budget my money, the sin budget will be my guideline."

"I don't get it. What do you mean by 'budget your sins!'" Millie questions.

Paula refreshes Millie's memory. "Remember? There are mortal sins, the really serious offences against the Ten Commandments. If you die without mortal sins being forgiven you go directly to hell. No passing 'GO.' No collecting $200. Then there are the venial sins, which are little offences against the Ten Commandments. If you die without having those forgiven in confession, you just go to purgatory. Your soul burns until it's pure enough to see God … more or less." Paula shrugs.  She knows Millie doesn't buy all her beliefs, but Millie always wants to compare them with her own.

Millie frowns as if to question, "If you say so! But what does all that have to do with the price of tea in China?"

"Take today for instance. I just got back from confession. My penance (cost) for having my sins forgiven is to say three 'Our Fathers,' three 'Hail Marys' and make a good 'Act of Contrition.' Not too bad. So, I figure if I can control what I say, how I say it and not swear too much - you know how fond I am of saying 'shit' and 'damn' – avoid arguing with Rusty and Annie, and back-talking Mr. Harper, I can keep my penance to three 'Our Fathers' and three 'Hail Marys.' If I go over that, then I'm out of control. But, I'll allow myself that much. That's where the budget comes in. How does that sound?"

"Complicated!" Millie ponders the proposition. After a few minutes she asks, "When do you leave?"

"Not sure. I'll have a test run the weekend after Easter. We'll leave from school on Friday. We have an arranged ride with a guy named Ed McElroy who works for Curtis Wright. He's Mr. Harper's neighbor at the lake. He provides transportation for Annie until school is out. Annie will give me the grand tour of the park. She says there are a couple of guys she has her eyes on for us to hang out with, so we'll check it out."

Millie mimics, "Oh, magosh! Don't forget to check out the guys! First things first and all that. Call me when you get back. I want every detail. ...every dot over the i's and every cross of the t's."

* * *

8

They turn the corner of Hill Place from Perry St., where both live at the dead end. Their bedrooms are about eight feet across from each other. They prayed together all through World War II, when everyone was uncertain what the future held. Paula goes to a Catholic private school and Millie goes to public school the same years that "Hop-along" Cassidy is the star football player for Central High where Millie attends.

As they reach home, Paula concludes, "I feel confident enough that my sin budget will keep me good enough not to give Mr. Harper too much trouble. Although Annie's family isn't Catholic, she's always attended Catholic schools, and Mr. Harper assures Mother he will make every provision for me to keep the rules and regulations such as mass on Sunday, no meat on Fridays and confession once a month. All agreements are made. The plans are about to be set in stone."

"You sure were right about having news. Talk to you later," Millie shouts as she goes up the steps to her porch.

* * *

After supper Paula daydreams about her imagined future, *it will certainly be a change from my life now. Just when life settles down and gets the least bit comfortable, something happens ... the big stir in the sky. Moral of the story – don't get too comfortable because for sure, it won't last.*

*I'll have to have a back-up plan. 'Don't put all your Easter eggs in one basket,' as the old saying goes.*

Paula recalls five years ago, when Millie's family invited her to spend a week of their vacation with them two years in a row. They rented a cottage at Fisher's Landing on the banks of Buckeye Lake. When entering from the driveway we came into a large kitchen with two bedrooms and a bath on one side. On the second floor was a large enough living room with two bedrooms on the side. Walking out to a screened-in porch, there it was, Buckeye Lake. It was so peaceful at night. Millie and Paula played "Go Fish" with a flashlight under the blankets. They talked and giggled about what Millie's brother and his friend did and said.

*My life at home was mostly strife – but at the lake, all we had to do was make our bed and set the table for dinner. I did the same at home but it was always in the midst of arguments about money, family needs and mother asking dad, 'Do you still love me?'*

* * *

Paula's mother had a habit of setting her up for punishment. One time, ten year old Paula was skating on the back sidewalk. She wanted to tighten her skates and then go to the front sidewalk to continue skating. She got her skate key from the nail behind the kitchen door. Paula told Mother, "I'll be out front skating."

Her mother answered gruffly, "I told you to stay in the back yard today, young lady."

The back walk stretches from the porch to the alley and is very narrow, bumpy and not good for roller skating. Paula finished adjusting her skate straps, then turned to the back door and stuck out her tongue in her mother's direction. She wasn't allowed to do that, or make snoots, talk back, or make any gestures like she'd seen other kids do.

Mother was waiting for Paula's response on the other side of the window curtain. That was one time Paula was grateful for her bobbed hair.

"Get in here, you insolent little bitch!" She grabbed Paula's hair to hurry her through the kitchen where she kept her handy yardstick. For many years Paula thought the sole purpose of the yardstick and the razor strap was to beat the

10

kids. However, neither her brother, Fred, nor her sister, Jeniece, ever got the yardstick that Paula could remember. It seemed just Paula's name was on it. Many days she went to school with welts on her legs from yard sticks, switches from the stink tree in the back yard or the strap. So, yes, she looked forward to a week's vacation with her neighbors.

* * *

After their chores at the lake house were done, the rest of the time was theirs to explore. They'd walk the train trestle barefoot to the general store in Millersport. The girls would buy something for their hope chest. Paula didn't know what she was supposed to put in the hope chest, but it seemed like the thing to do. Millie and Paula didn't want to spend too much money because they knew they'd have one day at the amusement park and one day for swimming at Crystal Pool. They'd always squeeze in some skee-ball games to add to their stack of tickets. The painted plaster of Paris dolls and stuffed animal prizes were coveted.

Of course, they used to worry the grownups about letting the girls take the rowboat out on the lake. Sometimes they'd fish from the pier. Back then it was common to catch 40 lb. catfish and carp that made your eyes bug out. The girls didn't catch them, but some of the men did. Millie saw pictures.

That was 1943 and 1944. World War II was going on and everyone's life was turned upside down. Shoes and certain foods were rationed along with gasoline and tires. Everyone was issued ration stamps that resembled postage stamps, 'Lick 'm and stick 'm.' Paula got to do that after she colored the Dixie Margarine yellow. It was white while in the store and it came in a one lb. brick like butter did along with a small pack of the yellow coloring. If Paula didn't color it, her mother would just put it on the table as it was. White! While saying, "Oleo is oleo." It looked like lard to Paula and she wouldn't eat it.

* * *

Paula remembers these special times. What will Buckeye Lake amusement park be like for a teenager without rations and looking for more special times? She can't wait to find out. Suddenly, life feels sweet. Paula's feeling on top of the world.

*I don't know Mr. Harper that well, but he likes me and I like his kids.*

It's hard not to sin when her mother sets her up for punishment. Especially now that she is fourteen and wants to flex her fourteen-year-old muscles.

Paula gives her situation some thought …*I spend a fair amount of time figuring out how I'm going to conduct myself. I guess I'll Just act normal and whatever happens because of it, I'll just have to take it and learn from it. Mother threatens to kill me on a regular basis but she hasn't. She just doesn't know how to get me to do what she wants me to do.*

*I really don't understand her. About two or three days a month I'd have just enough time to relax a little and think Mother really does like me a bit but just like foul weather, her personal storms seize the moment. I wish I knew when that was so I could prepare myself. I never really developed much trust for adults. Maybe that's why I  used to be so shy around them when I was little. I'd be surprised with a spanking and not understand why I was getting it.*

\* \* \*

Mrs. Bradley's head is forever looking over Paula's shoulder, reading her diary, and listening in on her telephone conversations – according to her, it's to keep Paula on 'the straight and narrow.' So, with Paula's 'sin budget' plan, all should work out for her.

Even though she's excited about the thoughts of spending a special summer and being 14 which carries its own specialness, she also feels something else down deep; ... an unnamed excitement. It feels like dancing is going on in her belly. Paula is also feeling a bit uneasy about the separation from her parents. She was separated once before and she thinks she is replaying that whole scenario of 1940.

\* \* \*

Paula had been in kindergarten for a half of a school year at age five. It was February because she remembers giving valentines. Her mother took her to her maternal grandmother's in the small town of Marysville, Ohio. She didn't give Paula an explanation as to why she left her with 'Mom' as Paula called her grandmother. Paula knew she was a source of friction between her parents. Her mother was widowed with six year old Fred when Paula's parents married. Her brother, as she calls him, seems to be the apple of everyone's eye, especially to her maternal grandparents. When Paula was born, Fred was nine. When Fred was 14 and Paula was five, Mother left her with 'Mom.'

Mom enrolled Paula in school. Since there was no kindergarten, she was put in the second half of first grade. She didn't know how to print yet like the other kids did. She couldn't read yet. She didn't know anyone and she had no idea why she was there. She felt very much alone. It was good that she loved Mom. Mom cut bangs which made Paula look cute. She bought her some cute clothes, new crayons and pencils and she helped Paula with reading. "Dick and Jane" was hard because Paula hadn't the benefit of the first half of first grade.

Paula overheard Mom asking the visiting church ladies one afternoon to pray for her parents. "They smoke, drink and fight."

Paula didn't know what to think but she was very sad, lonely and homesick. She loved her parents and Fred, but was sure they didn't love her. … Her parents did those bad things only some of the time.

It wasn't until late June, after school was out, that Mother showed up at Mom's. She was furious that Mom had cut bangs – "how dare you make decisions about Paula's hair. Now I have to look at it till those bangs grow out. One more thing for me to take care of." Mother said.

Mother's going to take Paula back home. Paula was both excited and scared at the same time. Mom and Paula got along fine. Mom liked her. Paula didn't know if mother was still the same.

That afternoon when Mother came to get her, Paula heard crying in Mom's bedroom. She went in to find the source. A baby was lying in a dresser drawer.

"Paula," Mother called as she brought in a stack of diapers, "This is your new baby sister, Jeniece."

Paula was stunned. Not only did she have a new baby sister but she was told that her family moved to Richmond, Indiana and she would be starting over in first grade when she turned six. Paula asked about her dog, who was her best friend in the whole world.

Mother said, as if she had just waved good-bye to a neighbor, "Your dog ran away." Paula's eyes started to tear-up. "We'll get another dog when we get moved."

\* \* \*

Paula told her dog everything. She had so much to tell him. How could she share all that had happened to a dog she didn't even know? She just couldn't sort anything out now. She felt replaced by a baby she didn't ask for either. It seems that everything that's happening is always about her folks. They give no thought to how Paula feels about anything. Mainly, Paula feels she's 'in the way.' She's just a kid, not a person who matters. *When will I be old enough to matter?* she wonders while still feeling stunned over the whole situation.

Enter, alter ego.

*I'll still be with you.* She hears a voice in her head. Paula looks around but doesn't see anyone.

"Who is here? Where are you? Paula asks hesitantly.

*Well, since you are fond of rabbits and dogs ... you might think of me as a lamb.*

"Where are you? I can hear you but I can't see you?"

*I'm like your imaginary playmate that you talk to when you play by yourself and talk to yourself ... I can hold all your secrets for you. You can tell me anything. You can talk to me with your thoughts. Try it. Just THINK what you want to say to me. Nobody but you can hear me. No one can see me. You will be able to feel my presence if I'm needed or wanted. Just call on me with your mind.*

*OK! Do you mean like this? Do you have a name?*

*Just call me 'Leonard.' How's that? I'm kind of like a guardian angel. You pray to me every night, don't you? ... to whom God's love, commits me here ... ' so here I am. ... Try not to worry too much. I know you are scared right now with all the new stuff that's happened to you. Remember, I am right with you and you can ask me anything or tell me anything.*

Paula forgets and says "OK" out loud and hopes no one sees the look that must be showing on her face.

Paula smiles to herself as she is remembering her introduction to Leonard, her alter ego or guardian angel. She's willing to forego questions.

* * *

Paula is really missing her dad and Jeniece. She knows Mother desperately wants to be with them. On the one hand, she's glad for Mother but also feeling guilty because Paula's planning a wonderful special summer. This time Paula is making it about herself. She supposes all this will sort itself out in time. Meanwhile, there are clothes to buy, kids to meet, exams to take and a new family to get used to living with. She always has the feeling of being outside of things. She learns a lot by observing.

# CHAPTER III
## ASSESSING THE WARDROBE

"For crying out loud, Mother, where do you find the shorts you pick out for me? Shorts have a style, you know. I want new ones with pegged legs and cuffs. I don't want Lana Turner, World War II, pleated shorts with four buttons on the front like sailors' front flaps. Did you buy me tap shoes to go with them?"

Mother gives Paula a disgusted look and replies, "No, Miss Smarty Pants. The shorts belonged to the neighbor across the alley. Some of her other clothes fit you and she thought they'd look nice on you."

Wise, Mother. Just because they look nice on me doesn't mean I should wear them. Why do you think she is weeding them out of her closet? It isn't because she's outgrown them now, is it? They are out of style. When I was in eighth grade you thought I looked nice in your remodeled plush coat that Betty Davis might have worn. You just can't go on embarrassing me like this. I don't want to stand out. I want to fit in. Do you think you might just try to understand that?"

Mother finally gives in. She takes thirty dollars out of an empty cigarette pack in the back of the Marlboro carton. "This is all I can spare right now. Make a list of what you need. Make it go as far as you can. You'll have to buy any extras you want out of your earnings. As far as this session goes, I've had enough. I'm going to put some Eight O'clock coffee on the hotplate. Where is the percolator?"

"It's in the clothes basket with the cake and pie pans." Paula points to a stack of blankets on top of the basket that hides its contents.

Mother says under her breath, "I'm going to listen to the radio. It's time for 'Ma Perkins' … then take a nap."

17

"Thanks, for the cash, Mother. I'll call Millie to see if she can go shopping with me."

\* \* \*

Paula goes to George's bedroom that used to be hers. She opens the window about a foot and a half. Millie's bedroom light is on. *She's probably pin-curling her hair for tomorrow. George will be home soon, so I'll have to hurry.* She told Mrs. Martin she has to use the bathroom. Since there is only one bathroom it has to be shared by the two families.

Millie comes to the window after Paula hits it with a tossed penny.

"You'd better stop throwing pennies on the bay window roof. If my little brother sees them, he won't be able to resist trying to get them. What's going on?"

"Can you come over? I need your help. I go to Buckeye Lake this weekend and I need to buy some clothes," Paula begs.

"Yes, but I can't stay too long. I have more homework to do." She puts her comb and brush in her dresser drawer and grabs a jacket.

"OK. Meet you downstairs." Paula says as she quickly closes the window, runs to the bathroom to flush the toilet so as to back up her story of having to use the bathroom. She nearly falls down the steps to let Millie in. They proceed to the new basement apartment, if you could call it that.

"Mother calls it 'cozy. I'm not allowed to say what I think it is … welcome to our new digs. To the left, see the blanket strung on strong clothes lines. Move the curtains and the washing machine and rinse tubs are handy. You'd think we are kids making a playhouse. I'm sorry we have to be down here," Paula apologizes. She pushes Millie down on the davenport. "Here's a tablet and pencil."

Millie struggles to sit up. "Whoa! Am I promoted to secretary? I haven't finished my shorthand class yet. Don't worry about your new digs. It's for what? Two months, Paula?"

"Yes, you are the secretary. Here's what's happening. Mother gave me $30.00 for my emergency summer wardrobe. Help me out, will you? You've got a way about getting down to business." Paula starts to dictate as Millie makes columns on the paper.

"OK!" Millie agrees. "Let's start with the train case."

Paula slaps her head with the heel of her hand. "Oh, magosh! I never even thought of the train case, the most basic and important item young girls have for overnights. See how flustered I am?"

Millie starts right in making a list . . . "a card of bobby pins, Breck shampoo, a bottle of Teel toothpaste, Kotex, a new sanitary belt. You are not spending more than $5.00 on that stuff, no matter what. That leaves $25.00. Where do we go from there?"

"Night, day, work, play, socks . . ." Paula's voice fades while she busies herself making a calendar in squares for a specific 'do-it' list.

Millie quickly adds, "Let's get your church clothes out of the way first. You ARE going to church this summer, aren't you?"

Paula cocks her head to the side, "Of course. Looks at Millie with a squint and says, "You really know how to reduce my clothes money. ... I have that full skirt I made in Home Ec class. - The one with the huge flowers on it. I'll wear that with my white nylon blouse. My garter belt is OK. I can use a new brassiere and one pair of stockings. I have a slip. That's enough for church. I need pajamas. I'll do with one new pair. Forget slippers."

As Millie writes, she says, "Gotcha! Brassiere, stockings, and pj's ... That brings us down to $21.00, more or less. I guess I can erase your flowered skirt off my list for borrowing."

"Sorry." Paula continues. "I want three pair of pegged, cuffed shorts - red, maybe blue, and gray ones with three buddy blouses to go with them."

"Boy, oh boy. We should have started with the new look first," Millie notes.

"It's going to be for work AND play, Millie. That leaves about $4.00 for socks and underpants. Want to meet me at Lazarus after school tomorrow?" Paula asks.

After checking her assignment book in the back pocket of her dungarees Millie says, "I can meet you, but I have to be home by 6:00 for my piano lesson."

"Tell you what. We'll start at Lazarus for the blouses, shorts and a Maiden form bra. '*I dreamed I went shopping in my Maiden form bra.*'" The girls both laughed. "Then we'll go to Woolworths five and dime for the rest. We'll save time and money that way. Of course, that's assuming we don't run into anybody we know who wants to play records in Lazarus' record shop. I'm counting on you to keep us on track, OK," Paula urges.

Shopping done! Train cases and battered suitcases are packed. Annie and Paula wait at Fifth Ave. and Nelson Rd. for Mr. McElroy. "I don't care if the sky IS grey and overcast. I just want to be there," Paula says.

"Anything you want to know about the lake, ask Mr. McElroy. He's the recognized historian/photographer of the area. He knows everybody." Annie assures Paula.

"Is that him at the gas station?" Paula points to the gas station.

Annie waved a hello. "Is that 'he' at the gas station?"

"You know what I mean. Stop correcting my grammar." Paula gently nudges Annie shoulder to shoulder.

Mr. McElroy promises, "There won't be much traffic at the lake today, so we'll make good time. In about two weeks when the regulars arrive, there will barely be room for your shadow."

"Paula's got more questions than Carters has liver pills. If it's OK, I'll put her in front with you and I'll nap in the back. I'll get a break from all the questions. I'm about out of answers anyway." Annie comments as she nudges Paula toward the front seat.

"Sure thing. Hop in. What would you like to know, Paula?"

"For starters," she asks, "Who are the 'regulars' I hear Annie talk about?"

He starts his spiel. "Some of the park folks like myself live here the year round. We are the regulars along with the 'carnies.' They come and set up their rides and concession stands. They paint, and hammer day and night to be ready for the park to open. If they need changes in their space, 'Whitie' says in his bass voice, 'Whadaya want?' They tell him. He builds it. Everybody's happy."

"Who is Whitie?" Paula continues questioning like she's going to be examined on the answers. She is used to A's.

"He's the park manager who's the 'Go Between' for Mr. Turner, the park owner, and the concession owners."

"So, go on. I want the whole story." Paula is hungry for all details.

"Then, the people arrive who live here all summer in their own cottages. They are regulars too. Their places have been boarded up for the winter. Pumps have to be primed, gas lines opened. Some folks still have outhouses AND a bathroom. The boat livery people have to update their paint jobs and signs. A lot has to be done before the park officially opens. Livery means boat rentals."

"I would never have thought about all that goes on to make the magic happen," Paula shook her head in disbelief.

He continues, "Most people don't. I talked to Ruth Caster at the Chamber of Commerce the other day. She said there's an uncommon amount of activity already for this time of year. She doesn't have that many openings available for new renters. Harper was lucky to get the cottage he got. My wife and I have three concessions of our own and we already have our signs repainted."

"What are your concessions?" Paula keeps her steady stream of questions going.

"We have skee-ball, popcorn, peanuts, salt water taffy, and a kiddie ride."

"You have to take care of all that yourselves?"

"Well, the kids are old enough to help now. They make sure the kiddie-boats are running properly such as no loose bolts or nuts as well as touch up paint and new signs for the ride. They also compare the supply list with the supplies we receive to make sure we are ready with all the food supplies we need well before opening day. … All your questions are helping me, Paula. I'm making my 'do it' list while I'm telling you." He gives a brief laugh and says, "Continue …"

Paula tells him, "Ruth Caster is my aunt's friend. I suppose she'll be looking over my shoulder this summer since I'll be living with the Harpers."

"Well, honey, it's like this. When the park gets busy and the kids run with lots of spare time on their hands, the park people keep an eye out on ALL the kids. They care as much about my kids as their own. I care just as much about theirs as I do mine. We don't want anything harmful to happen to any of you. So don't see it as us being nosy. Think of it as a safety issue. We all have to cooperate. It gets too busy and there are too many strangers. Even some we know are a bit unsavory. We're mindful."

Paula noticed that route 40 went through 'one horse' towns foreign to her.

He asks," Where are you going to work, Paula? I take pictures of the entire area. I'll probably come around and snap a picture of you too, if you like."

"Mr. Harper said that after Annie shows me how to shave ice for making snowballs without losing my fingers, spin sugar for the cotton candy, and run the cash register, I'll be working next to the pier ballroom at his snowball stand. I don't know where any of that is yet."

From the backseat, Annie says, "We really wanted to work together. Daddy just laughed. He says he knows better than that."

Paula glances out the window. She notices they'd been driving an hour and a half. Nothing is happening. Nothing! There's barely a car on the main drag. They passed a small grocery store and dry cleaner on the way in. The only thing that relieved the monotony of the drive were the Burma Shave signs. "If hugging on the highway - - is your sport - - trade in your car - - for a davenport - - Burma Shave."

The trees are just beginning to sprout. Mr. McElroy's '47 Packard finally pulls up in front of Mr. Harper's small white rental cottage. *Our street has gravel on it. It feels good to call it 'our street.' Mr. Harper isn't going to have any trouble with me at all. The tires make a comfortable sound on the gravel along with the whirr of the car's motor. It won't be any-time at all before I can tell who is coming and going by the sound of the motor and the time of day.*

When he comes to a stop the girls get out and grab their bags. "Bye, Mr. McElroy. Thanks for the ride. See you Monday morning." they call as he backs out of the driveway.

"6:00 sharp. Call me Ed," he waves as he drives off.

\* \* \*

Paula mentally assesses what she observes. *There's still a bite in the air and no foliage to break the wind. A large tree stands to the west of the house. A hint of a gravel driveway is to the east of the house. To the rear, where there might have been a garage stands a small paintless weathered structure that looks like an outhouse. What are we in for? The houses are so close together. I just can't get a feel for anything. There's no traffic, no people, no kids, no lights, no parked cars and after entering the house, maybe no heat and maybe, no supper.*

\* \* \*

Annie opens the front door without a "Hi."

Paula says, "Just like home. No need for a key. Three houses off the main highway. I guess there's no one around to intrude."

They've got suit cases, train cases and book bags.  For the weekend Paula unpacks her black and white Spaulding saddle oxfords, a brown skirt, a blue scotch nap sweater, white cardigan and two blouses plus her blue jeans.

Mr. Harper pulls onto the gravel driveway with Rusty in tow. They unload groceries and their suit cases. Paula runs to the door to meet them and help carry bags of food and supplies. She makes a relay chain stationing Annie in the kitchen to figure out where to put all the items as she unpacks.

Hamburger, buns, a chicken, some potatoes, eggs, cereal and milk.

Mr. Harper brings in the last of the grocery bags. "It won't be a fancy feast, but it will get us through the weekend and then I'll have time to get the house organized. You girls make a house and grocery list. I'll have things ready for the move -in!"

While he busily fries hamburgers, the girls prepare the trimmings for supper. Rusty disappears to his bedroom to unpack some toys and comic books.

"Have a good trip out, girls?"

"Yes," Annie answers." Mr. McElroy filled Paula in on the ways of the local folks.

"Welcome home, Paula. Once the park opens, we'll take a lot of our meals there and you won't see that much of the house."

Aware of her mother's absence, Annie says, "Paula takes Home Ec so she and I can fix dinners at home too."

"Lots of homework?" Mr. Harper asks.

"Some – enough. A little Latin to translate. Caesar just doesn't interest me," swoons Annie.

*"Veni, Vidi, Vici*!" Paula adds. "That pretty much says it all.

Paula is looking everything over. The house is meagerly furnished. She tries to get an impression. It's like a blank book waiting to be written in. A calendar on the wall reads September, 1948. Behind Rusty's room is Mr. Harper's bedroom with a double iron bed which holds a bare mattress and springs, a tall dresser and flowered paper on the walls. There is a framed picture of a bunch of dogs playing poker. She remembers the party that her aunt Esther gave for 'our boys' after the war ended. Paula smiles. Behind the living room is a hidden stairway that creates a bridge of some sort that either goes down on the other side to the dining room or to a finished half story making a left turn at the landing leading up. Hmmm! One can get upstairs from the living room or the dining room. The small dining room has a table for six and a sideboard. The overhead light with a pull chain is handy. She has never seen a floor plan like this. She really likes what she sees. There are five chairs and number six is in the living room. The kitchen has a wide porcelain sink, a small refrigerator and a work surface on top of a washstand with drawers and a side door for pans. Back in the corner is a washing machine. The bathroom is beside the stair steps. The tub has familiar ball and claw feet, just like at home.

"Ouch!" Paula hears Annie moan as she goes up the stairs. "How tall are you, Paula?"

Paula sings, "5 foot 2, eyes of blue, but oh what these five feet can do."

"I cracked my head going up the stairs so be sure to duck at the top," Annie warns.

It is a half story with pale green Kemtone paint on the walls and a floral congoleum rug on the floor. The room still has a slight musty smell which should disappear in time with a good airing out.

\* \* \*

Annie rejoins the first floor activity of meal making. She says, "Daddy, after supper can I show Paula the ball field while there's still light out?"

"That's a good idea. Heh! Heh! Nice try, girls. The dishes can wait till you get back. Say, around 9:00?"

"Agreed," Annie answers.

"Thanks, 'Mr. Daddy,'" Paula says as she goes around the table and gives him a big hug.

26

\* \* \*

After supper, they change from their school uniforms to dungarees and saddles. They grab their school sweaters and poplin windbreakers then head out the door.

Rusty hands Paula a softball as the girls pass him. He's content to listen to "Superman" and "Jack Armstrong, the All American boy" on the radio while his dad reads the *Newark Advocate* and the *Columbus Citizen.*

Annie tells Paula en route, "Last week there were kids at the ball field. It's only a couple blocks over. It's really just a vacant lot where the kids get together and play ball."

Paula looks around with disappointment. "No one is here but us. We might as well make the best of it and toss a few balls to each other."

"I guess no one is going to show up tonight." Annie responds with a look of disappointment. "Uh oh! Look North."

Two guys come toward them. 'Red Hat' has a ball and glove. 'Blue Plaid Coat' has a bat. Paula's heart starts racing. 'Red Hat' tosses a ball to Annie as they near her. The boys met her earlier this week, Paula discovers. Annie misses the catch. Paula picks the ball up and throws it to 'Plaid Coat.' Annie trips over a small log. The guys rush to help her up.

"Just like gym class," Paula says. The guys laugh at Annie.

"Thanks," Annie says as she picks herself up and brushes herself off. "This is Paula, my school friend. She will be staying with us for the summer."

Like a bunch of kindergarten kids the boys say in a sing song voice, stretching it out, "Hi, Paula."

"Red Hat looks at Paula and says, "I'm Breck. This is my friend, Chip. This is where you say 'Hi!' Chip."

27

As Chip grabs Breck's red leather hat and swats him
with it, he smiles at the girls, nods his head and says "Hi."

They walk farther into the field. "How about some 'first
bounce or a fly?'" Breck calls.

The four of them take positions. Chip hands Annie the
bat. After about ten of Breck's pitches she finally hit a fly
ball.

"Got it! Got it! Got it!" Chip calls as he catches the ball.

Annie hands the bat to Chip and takes to the field.

"Chuck it to me," Chip calls, exercising the bat with a
few practice swings. Breck pitches.

Chip hits the ball far and wide.

"Wow!" Paula hollers. "You can really hit that ball!"
She drools over him. He's very good looking. Black curly
hair, dimples, white gorgeous teeth, low voice and the most
beautiful blue eyes, she is smitten already!

When Chip hits one directly to Paula, she catches it and
goes up to bat while Annie and Breck call "Way to go!"

Breck and Annie come in closer. Chip takes the ball to
pitch. "Where do you want it?"

Paula shows him. He put it right where she says. Soft
balls and Paula are no strangers. She sends it sailing toward
imaginary first base. Breck stumbles over Annie and catches
the ball. "OK – I'll have my turn at bat." he calls.

"You don't need a turn. Fifteen minutes is enough," Chip
moans. "Let's go to the Bus Station. It's getting too dark to
see the ball anyway."

Paula looks at Annie to see if she is in agreement.

"Sure. But we have to be home by 9:00, more or less.
We still have to unpack school stuff, ... you know,
homework." she says.

"Why would we go to the Bus Station?" Paula wants to
know.

"It's the place where the kids hang out," Breck says
matter of factly.

"Who will be there?" she continues with the questions as they walk four abreast, switching places from time to time as they go.

"Whoever shows up," Chip cuts in.

"So what will we do there? My picture of a bus station is a place where you can buy a ticket and sit in pews while waiting for the bus."

"Nah! It's like a diner – food, pop, snacks, newspapers, magazines and bus tickets to 'New-Ark,'" Breck recites, emphasizing Newark to sound like New York.

Breck and Chip laugh and punch each other. They had heard a lady ask the bus driver if he was going to 'New Ark.'

"I don't get it," Paula says. "Where is the bus station anyway? I didn't see one when we drove in today."

"It's catty- wompus from the park entrance," Breck says.

"Route 79 comes in from Hebron and makes a right turn at the park entrance and continues on to Millersport," Chip adds.

"This looks like a drug store." Annie says.

"You got it!" Breck holds the door open and waits for Annie to go first.

Chip then takes the door for Paula. "Head for a booth," he says.

Each red Naugahide booth looks like it could fit eight snugly. They appear to be well used. "The first one has a rip," Annie says. "Let's take the next one."

The stainless steel center pillar holds a grey marble looking formica table top with a stainless steel rim around it. The back of the seats are padded and have spaced buttons made to look like smocking.

"You two get in first," Chip shoves playfully.

"There aren't any other kids here. Some hangout!" smirks Paula.

Annie looks a bit concerned, "I hope you guys have some money. We didn't come prepared for treats."

Breck and Chip empty their pockets. Chicklets, gum wrappers, a pocket knife, a restroom token from somewhere, a pair of tweezers and a shooter. Lo and behold, some change! They shove it together to the middle of the table. "Fifty cents. That should do it." Chip says to the waitress, "Four large fountain Cokes, please."

"Make mine lemon, please," Paula requests.

"That's my mom," Chip says.

"Why didn't you introduce us?"

"I don't know if I want her to know who you are." went the banter. They all laugh.

The group continues to talk among themselves while waiting for their Cokes. Chip looks up as the door opens. "Oh, there's Debby Jackson and her old man."

She doesn't want to sit in a booth with him, Paula observes, then comments to Chip, "Seems to be some tension between them."

"Her mother wears the combat boots," Chip agrees. "She probably sent Debby to the bar to tell her dad to come home to supper."

"Shh!" says Breck as he scootches down in the booth, "I don't want her to see me."

Chip says, "She's Breck's girlfriend."

"Not anymore," says Breck from under the table.

"Does she know it yet?" Chip is laughing.

Debby and her dad leave. The door opens again.

"Hey, Double Jay. Come sit with us." Breck calls.

"Hi, guys! You seen my pal?" Jay asks,

"Not so far – speak of the devil -" Chip motions to the door as another guy enters.

"Why is he called 'Double Jay'?" Annie asks.

"Both of them are Jays."

Chip adds, "They are best friends. You seldom see one without the other."

J1 got up to meet J2. They exchange words and make some hand gestures. Suddenly, J2 says to J1, "Go ya to the booth!"

The race was on. They shoved chairs and each other out of the way in a mad scramble for the booths. J2 beat J1, hands down.

Chip's mother returned to get the Jay's orders. "What'll you have, boys?" she asks.

"Two beers."

"Sure you will." Chip's mother just shakes her head as she walks off.

"Don't they care how long we sit here?" Paula worries, as she finishes her coke.

"As long as we buy something - pew rent, I guess." Breck offers.

Laughter and joking travels fast in the booth.

Chip's mom comes back with two root beers and tosses a large bag of chips on the table. "On the house." She says.

The Jays say in concert, "Thanks Mrs. Austin.

All are introduced and everyone catches up on the news and no news. The J's finish their drinks and get up to leave.

Breck says, "Singing J1, Come by the house tomorrow. Maw-doo baked cookies."

Jay 1 responds, "Maw-doo Dempsy bakes the best cookies."

"Why did Breck call him 'Singing J1?'" Paula whispers to Chip.

"J1 sings barbershop with his dad and brothers. They sing at church and around."

"I sing with them sometimes," Breck adds.

"Do you sing too, Chip?" Paula asks him.

"Only in the shower."

"Where do they sing on Sunday?" Annie wants to know.

"At the Community Church on Picnic Point," Breck fills in.

31

After finishing their Cokes and ice, they leave the extra 10 cents on the table for a tip. Chip waves "Bye" to his mom. Then Chip asks, "You girls want our 'two-bit tour' of the park tomorrow?"

Paula looks at Annie and hopes she'll go for the offer.

"I'm sure Dad will go along with the tour if we get our chores done. Say, about 11:00?" Annie answers enthusiastically.

"Business seems to be picking up. Who is the young dirty faced kid in the torn shirt and the big shoes with no socks or laces?" Paula leans toward Chip while Annie and Breck are bantering. The kid looks to be six or seven years old. She watches him as her group scramble out of the booth, looking like midgets getting out of a Crosley.

Chip tells Paula, "That's Davie, the Gypsy boy."

Paula whispers to Chip, "Davie paid for a pack of Luckys and put a Clark bar in his pocket."

"Yeah, well, sometimes he pays; sometimes not. If they catch him, he puts it back." Chip shrugs. "Nobody much cares."

Breck says, "Great! You two pick me up then the three of us will round up Chip by 11:15."

All are in agreement. The girls just need Mr. Harper's OK. Annie cautions, "If we aren't there by 11:10, you'll know we aren't coming,"

Annie and Paula enter the house by the stroke of nine. Mr. Harper nods and says, "Shh! Walter Winchell's news program just came on."

"Let's get the dishes washed and we'll ask Daddy when the commercials come on."

The musical jingle plays on the radio. "Nickle! Nickle! Ta roody ah – da da. Nickle! Nickle! Ta roody ah - da da. Pepsi-Cola hits the spot. 12 full ounces that's a lot. Twice as much and better too. Pep-si Cola is the drink for you!"

The girls sing and dance with the jingle. They get his attention and permission.

"Who'd you say wants to show you the park?" quizzes Mr. Harper.

"Chip Austin. His mother works at the bus station. And Breck Dempsy."

"Oh! I know Breck's dad, Virgil. He owns a Chris Craft. Docks it in a boathouse down the towpath. OK. I just don't want you hanging out with any riffraff."

Paula can't stop talking about the evening's events, "I'm getting a feel for the place and love every minute of it. What's a towpath?" she asks as they stumble up the stairs.

"I don't know. Save your questions for the guys," Annie says as she opens the window a couple inches. "Ah! a gentle breeze. The room still smells stuffy from being closed up all winter."

They make up the bed and hang their clothes.

"Last one in bed's a 'Mick,'" Paula calls.

She's a 'Mick' anyway, but Annie joins in the tussle. Irish Catholics are derogatorily referred to as 'Micks.'

"I don't want to be a 'Mick'," Annie squeals.

"Pipe down up there," Mr. Harper calls.

"Could you ask for a more perfect day?" Paula yawns.

"I can't believe it. See you in the morning. Night."

Annie was practically asleep already, but Paula's mind keeps going back to Davie, the Gypsy and Debby Jackson, Breck's former girlfriend. "Dear Guardian Angel, watch over him and her, and all of us for that matter. Amen."

Sleep comes quickly.

# Chapter V
## Two-Bit Tour

Annie and Paula arrive promptly at Breck's house for the 11:00 a.m. "two-bit tour."

Breck introduces the girls to his mother. She is pleasant enough, giving each a couple of her freshly baked oatmeal cookies to tide them over, whatever that means. The girls give thanks to Mrs. Dempsy. Breck makes "shush" motions like they shouldn't talk too loud.

His dad is an engineer on the railroad had just made a night run. Now is his sleeping time. Paula later discovers that this is more often the case than not. "Shh! Whatever you are doing, 'don't,' or 'do it someplace else.'"

"Maw-doo, I told Singing J to stop by for cookies," Breck says quietly as they leave.

Paula asks Breck, "Why do you call her Maw-doo?"

"Oh, I don't know. I called her that when I was a baby. Still do. She likes it. It's our little thing, you know."

Chip is waiting for them when they arrive.

Breck and Chip talk about the Bounds Addition and the Neel Addition and a couple other additions.

"What does that mean?" Paula makes a face. She's recognizing the need to learn a whole new vocabulary.

Chip explains, "Most of the people don't own the land they live on. They might own the house, but they lease the land."

As they walk, Breck is quick to add, "The price of leasing land added to the price they pay to rent a cottage makes the difference between renting and not renting. That's why it's important to know your additions and subtractions."

Paula asks Chip, "How long has he been like this?"

"Ever since I've known him. You learn to live with it," Chip answers as he helps Paula cross the highway.

Breck begins tour guiding as he takes Annie by the elbow and herds the other three together. "We are walking on Hebron Road. That small house across the road is the Chamber of Commerce. People who want to rent cottages start there. They are referred to owners who list their rentals with the Chamber of Commerce."

Paula says, "That's where Ruth Caster works. She's a friend of my Aunt Esther's. When 'our boys' came home after the war, Aunt Esther, who owns a tavern in Columbus, thought it would be fun to rent a cottage for a long weekend of poker playing, beer drinking, joke telling and nonstop picnic food. That would be a good celebration for 'our boys.' Although she never had any kids of her own, the sons and daughters of her patrons are always referred to as 'our' boys or girls."

Breck says, "Well, then, you've got a head start. I didn't know who the head of the Chamber is."

Farther down the highway, they come to the entrance of the amusement park. There is a structure that reminds Paula of a wind mill without the blades.

"That's the water tower," Chip says. "My mom works part time at Williams Restaurant across the street and part time at the Bus Station. My sister works there too. She and mom live together, but I live with my dad, step mother and step brothers and sisters."

They walk up a slight incline. A fair sized parking lot is on the right. Jukebox music is playing.

Annie hears, "Slow Boat to China" and asks, "Where is the jukebox?"

"That's the 'Pinkie.'" Chip answers. "The Pink Elephant is a night club. I think it was originally a dance hall or maybe a skating rink. Anyway, that's where the vacationers drink when they aren't drinking in their cottages."

"Where do the regular people drink and play cards if they don't do it in the Pinkie?"

Breck picks up where Chip leaves off. "Oh, they go to the Tavern. The lake people don't mix with the vacationers. The folks who live here year round are just regular private working folks. They do their job, have families and do all the things people in Columbus do. The vacationers lead different lives while they are here."

Paula utters, "Breck seems to have a good sense of what the 'Lake' is all about." Annie nods her head in agreement.

Chip continues their education as they pass the carousel. "'The Sidewalks of New York' is competing with 'A Slow Boat to China.'"

"Yeah! The vacationers are interested in renting boats, drinking, buying bait, drinking, getting their boats repaired, drinking, the best place to go swimming or fishing, and dating somebody they shouldn't be dating. They also want to know 'where's the ice house, where to buy liquor and last of all, what time is mass on Sunday?"

The carousel is playing the calliope tune heard at the circus. Something about the gladiators. Even though nothing is open for business yet, workers are tightening bolts, using oil cans and hammers to get ready for opening day on Easter Sunday. The sounds add excitement in the air.

As they walk by the open door of the Pinkie, Paula gets a big whiff of stale beer and cigarette smoke. She closes her eyes. "I can hear the voices at Aunt Esther's, talking about their problems and 'did you hear the one about the farmer's daughter?' and the latest moron joke. It's a comforting sensation. My folks spent Friday and Saturday nights there, coming home in between, of course. Mother plays euchre and Dad helps solve the problems of the world with one of his 'know-most-everything' friends."

Paula nods her head, "Yes, Aunt Esther's Tavern is the neighborhood 's Pinkie. Her place is 'information central.'"

Breck asks, "Who is this Aunt Esther anyway? You talk about her a lot."

Annie checks out what she thinks she knows about Paula's family. "Isn't she your dad's sister? Are they the ones who played Snuffy Smith and the revenuers in Perry County during prohibition?"

Paula laughs, "Well, you might say that. Dad made moonshine. He and Uncle Hite, Aunt Esther's husband, sold it in small towns around. They were never big time, I don't think. I did hear though that dad's baby sister's brother-in-law did get caught up in the revenuers' trap. He is still in the 'cooler.' They don't talk about it much. I just put the bits and pieces together when I hear them talking."

After they pass the Pinkie, they turn left. Breck hawks, "Here we have the Midway. Step right up ladies and gentlemen. Try your pitching arms. Knock down stacks of milk bottles, shoot the ducks, throw the basketball, step into the Penny Arcade, play skee-ball, collect those tickets to win yourself a plaster of Paris kewpie doll or a panda bear."

"My gosh! Is that where you'll be working this summer?" Annie asks.

"No. I'll work on Playland Pier. We'll come to that."

Annie asks Chip, "Will you be working in the park?"

"No. I help with my brothers and sisters at home. My dad and step mom have four little ones, and I help out in the mornings."

Chip points to the right, "And here is the world famous BUG next to the Flying Airplane, Ferris Wheel and the Dive Bomber. This large grassy plot is where the Free Act performs."

"What's the Free Act?" Paula wants to know.

"The park manager hires different acts to perform every day at 8:30 PM and 11:00 PM plus a 2:30 show on Saturday and Sunday afternoons. The "Flying Walendas," tight-rope walkers, animal acts and magicians. They play music and announce over a loud speaker who is playing. It draws the crowd to the Midway where they buy Yontz's frozen custard – the best in the world. Once you taste it, you are hooked. Among the other typical carnival food, drinks and rides, folks play the games on the Midway."

"What is a Midway anyhow?" Paula asks. "I don't know any of these terms."

Breck said, "It's a place half-way between one place and another."

At this point, Chip grabs Breck's red leather hat and swats him on the back with it. They both laugh. Paula is beginning to wonder if either of them has a serious bone in his body.

"Are you putting us on or being serious?"

Annie whispers to Paula, "They are full of it. But more importantly, though, they seem like the best of friends."

Breck says, "Well, if it isn't J1, not to be confused with J2. Hey, Jay! Where you headed? Did you get your cookies?"

Hi's were exchanged. "Yeah! Your mom makes the best oatmeal cookies, bar none."

41

"Where's J2?" Chip asks.

"He'll meet me here later. My aunt hired me to work at the fun house this summer. J2's gonna help me today."

J1 looked at the girls. "Who are you besides Annie and Paula?"

Annie says, "I moved here. My last name is Harper. Paula is staying with my family for the summer ... and her last name is Bradley. ... What's your last name?"

"'One' and my pal's last name is 'two.'"

The girls shake their heads and roll their eyes. "We asked for that one."

Breck butts in, "We're giving them our two-bit tour of the park."

J1 says to the girls, "Come by the 'Pretzel' when the park opens and I'll treat you to a ride."

"What kind of pretzel is it?" Paula wants to know. "I love big pretzels."

They all thought that was very funny.

"What?" she asks, "Did I say something wrong?"

Chip says, "It's a fun house called the 'Pretzel' because you ride through it in little cars on mini train tracks and the cars twist and turn."

J1 adds, "Couldn't have said it better. Don't tell anymore or it won't be fun."

Breck urges, "We'd better get on with the tour or we won't be finished before supper."

They pass the Midway and come to the "Dips."

"Well," Paula's eyes brighten. "This doesn't need any explanation. Is it a good roller coaster?"

"Best in these parts, I'm told," says Chip. "Don't touch 'em myself."

"Will you guys take us for our first ride?" asks Annie.

Breck says, "I suppose."

"I'll buy my own ticket. It would just be nice to go with someone who knows the dips."

"You got a deal." The guys agree.

Paula says, "By the way, Breck. About your name? Is it short for Brecktor, Breckfry, Brekster, or maybe after the wealthy and titled Englishman, Lord Breckington?"

"Actually, Mother was sure she was going to have a girl with beautiful hair. Breck shampoo had just come out and she loved it. She started referring to her baby as the 'baby Breck girl.' When I turned out not to be a girl, she had referred to me so often as Breck, she decided it sounded good, so Breck it's been ever since. No trouble till it came time for baptism. That's a story for another time."

"I never knew and never thought to ask." Chip looks to the heavens.

"Oh, here is my favorite place in the park, the skating rink." Annie cooed.

"That's just a pickup place," Breck retorts with a disgusted look.

"We just really love to skate," Paula says with a look of disapproval. "Are we having our first argument?"

Chip quickly moved the subject to himself. "I can just about manage to walk. Wheels! I pass."

They round the contour of the "Little Lake" where people rent little boats guided by chains and gears under water so parents don't have to worry about the little ones.

"Isn't it amazing how people get named?" Chip pokes fun at Breck. "On the right side of this wide tarmac path is a miniature golf course and Crystal Swimming Pool. I'll whip you any day of the week if you'd like to try playing golf instead of skate," Chip continues.

"You're on!" Even though Paula didn't know how to hold a golf club, she really likes Chip. "It looks like fun."

He hangs back to walk with her while Breck and Annie take the lead.

"And, ladies and gents, immediately in front of you across from Clay's restaurant is the world famous 'Star Boat Line' with Chris Crafts so fast they are guaranteed to spray water skiers as far away as Millersport. But, the boats aren't as good as my dad's Chris Craft," Breck brags.

Paula rolls her eyes and looks at Chip, "Is he for real?"

Chip shakes his head "yes" about the boat in question.

"We need to take a left here to cross the footbridge. The "little lake" is separated from Buckeye Lake proper." They show the flood gate that controls the water level of the little lake. Paula doesn't understand it but she will in time.

"You guys really know a lot about this place. Have you always lived here?" Paula asks.

Breck says, "I've lived here only three or four years but they are the important ones. I'd really miss it if I had to leave."

The boys showed them the Community church where J1 sings with his family.

Chip offers up a sweeping gesture toward the land mass.

"There are picnic tables, a shelter house and an out - house. People reserve Picnic Point for company picnics, reunions and "Colored Day." The 'Coloreds' get one day a year when they get to do everything that isn't closed down. Last year they closed the pool, the pier ballroom and the skating rink."

Of course Paula needs to know the whys and what fors.

Chip says, "I think they did it for crowd control. It's never been stated exactly. Those places were open a couple of years ago. Some regulars came in. One of the Colored fellas resented that they didn't get the day to themselves as advertised. The result was a fight which ruined a good time for everyone. There had been an understanding that no white folks would be welcome. From then on the park closed those places where there would be a crowd. That was the park's way of not spelling it out in so many words. They are hoping it continues to work. In the 'North' we don't segregate like they do in the 'South' but that's the park's way of segregating, I guess."

Breck kicked a clump of dirt, "Huh! I never really thought about it. Our family just stayed home."

They were all quiet for a while. They seemed to be considering Chip's reasoning. Nobody asked how he knew. Nobody asked if he saw it written someplace.

They head back to the willow at the footbridge that returns them to the park proper.

Paula notices that the bath house at Crystal Pool is two stories tall. "That's interesting. Does someone dive from the second floor into a damp sponge?" Paula smiles at her own attempt at humor.

Breck says, "That's Crystal Ball Room upstairs. The tickets are so much a dance. I guess maybe ten cents. Sometimes they have a live band and sometimes it's just jukebox music. I really haven't been there yet. When I do, I'll let you know the details."

Paula adds "My cousin talks about coming here from Somerset on a Saturday night. They have a place in Somerset called the 'Little Phil.' but you have to be old enough to drink before they let you in to dance. That must be why they come over here."

Annie also adds," I think there's a group every Saturday night coming from Somerset. Maybe you'll see her. Only problem is, when someone we know shows up, we still have to work."

"And on the right we have the Gypsy Tea Room," Breck continues. It's just a Quonset hut. They tell your fortune and if you believe it, I have a bridge you might like to buy. They have another place at the quiet end of the park that's owned by a couple of guys from New York or New Jersey. I don't know which. You can sort that out later."

"Are you serious? I've always been fascinated by the Gypsies. Are they related to Davie? I've read about them in books," Paula gushes.

"Davie is their little brother," Annie says. "I like their brother, Reon. He runs the High Striker. Ring the bell with the hammer, win a prize. He also guesses women's weight."

Chip adds, "Well, there's lots of stories and warnings – take little Davie for example. He seems to be fending for himself most of the time, but when the park is open, he is in and out of his sister's fortune telling hut like a yo-yo. I think they keep track of him with their crystal ball."

He and Breck laugh their heads off. "Again, I hold all they say at bay until I have time to check it out for myself. That's who I am," says Breck.

They finally arrive at "Playland Pier" where Breck will work this summer cooking French fries and making fish sandwiches.

Chip says, "I can almost smell the fries. You'll learn to love malt vinegar on them, if you don't already."

"I never heard of putting vinegar on fries. Where's your dad's place, Annie?"

"Farther down the tow path," she answers.

"What's a tow path?"

Breck, quick with an answer of course, "It's the place where all burned, stubbed and amputated toes are embedded. Ha ha ha."

"No," says Chip. "It's where the flat boats carried goods and groceries to folks who lived on the Ohio-Erie Canal connection."

"The lake was a link in the canal system. A couple of people on land would tow a boat full of groceries and supplies and somebody on the boat had a pole to keep the boat from running into the shore. They were headed to Millersport and beyond. Sometimes they used horses or mules to tow the boats."

Paula looks at Annie. Annie shakes her head, 'Yes.' So Paula let it rest. "Amazing!" Paula says after a while.

They eat their cookies and agree that the 'two bit tour' is concluded. "As soon as the park opens, you'll have tons more questions. This is all you get for twenty-five cents, though." Breck put a period at the end of the tour. Chip flips him a quarter.

Humming begins.

*"...hmm hmm. Watch the curves that fill the tunnel...* *hmm hmm!"* Paula likes Breck's singing while they head back home.

## CHAPTER VI
## MOVE IN AND HOW IT WORKS

With classes and exams finished Paula is excited to begin the next chapter of her adventure. Her dad makes the trip to Columbus to personally deliver her to Mr. Harper at Buckeye Lake. Annie, waiting since early morning, plans to introduce Paula to her favorite people before they have to help open the stands for the first full day.

The two fathers meet for the first time. They head to the park on their own so that Pete Bradley gets a feel for what Paula's days will be like. Bob Harper wants to assure him that Paula will be safe and well looked after.

Paula is about to have her firsthand experience with the carnies and concessionaires looking out for everyone's kids. Annie tells Paula that she will soon learn to weave herself in and around, and under the binoculars and spyglasses.

"I want to meet the Gypsies," Paula told Annie right at the start.

"You don't let go of the Gypsies, do you? I'll introduce you to my favorite, Reon. His sisters are the ones who read palms." Annie informs.

"I want my palm read." Paula pleads.

"Not today. I don't know if they'll do it for anyone under 16 anyway. Let's just start with Reon, if you don't mind." Annie shoves Paula along. They have a lot of things to accomplish today.

Paula catches a chubby guy in bib overalls with the corner of her eye. "Who is that?"

"Well, you aren't supposed to have anything to do with him."

"Why not?" Paula persists while trying to keep up with Annie.

"He has 'shiffless' and it's contagious." Annie makes her voice stern but not loud enough for anyone else to hear.

"What's 'shiffless?' I've never heard of so much stuff that's out here. I have never been vaccinated, you know. With all the different schools I went to in first grade I managed to miss the needle. Should I get one here?" Paula earnestly questions.

"I don't know for sure what it is other than you aren't supposed to get it. I think it causes blindness. I'll ask Daddy if you need to get vaccinated," comforts Annie.

They round the corner at the drugstore. Moving right along past the Star Boats the smell of waffles drifts in on the occasional breeze.

"Enough said." Paula shrugs.

"There's Reon at the high striker. Look back over your left shoulder. Let's go back and say 'Hi!'"

They head towards the entrance of Playland Pier where Reon has his guessing game.

"Hi, Reon." Meet Paula. She's living with us and working for my dad this summer."

"Annie! Paula! Glad to meet you. Wanna ring the bell with the hammer?" Reon offers.

"Hi, Reon. I don't think I could. I'm not strong enough," Paula backs up.

"Just give it a try. Good advertising. People see you trying and they are sure they can do better. Here. Have a go at it," Reon urges.

Paula can barely lift the hammer. It almost knocked her backwards as she pulled the hammer behind her head. …
WHAM!

"I can't believe I only raised the striker to 20." Paula lets out a huff and steps backward.

Reon takes the hammer from Paula. "Wanna try, Annie?"

"No. I'll do it later. We have to open the snowball stand. Paula has a lot to learn today." Annie gently takes her friend by the arm and directs her back to the path.

Paula calls over her shoulder, "Bye, Reon. See you around. I'll practice getting some muscle."

As they walk away, Paula tells Annie, "He seems easy to talk to."

Annie lowers her voice. "Reon is very nice. Polite. I guarantee that you won't know any more about him by the end of summer than you know right now."

As they pass the Quonset hut, Paula sees two women in the 'tea room.' "One looks like she's expecting a visit from the stork."

"They probably both are," Annie responds.

"My mother told me about Gypsies in Marysville, Ohio when she was a girl. She said they'd leave a mark at friendly places when they caravanned through town. She wasn't supposed to let them see her because they steal little girls and chickens."

"Good combination," Annie commented. "I don't suppose they eat the baby girls."

"Mother said the Gypsies feel entitled to take whatever they want as their own. That's their way. ... I wonder if the Gypsies have to have special permission to live and work here for the summer."

Annie ponders. "I'm not sure. Never thought about it. After the park closes, it's my understanding that they go back east. Maybe New Jersey. Isn't that where Coney Island is?"

Paula's mind keeps going from one thought to another. "I don't know. ... Anyway, I'm so glad to be done with school for the summer. I know it was hard on Mother yesterday while she helped me pack. She acted a little sore at me. I think she had mixed feelings about letting Dad drive me without her."

"It was swell of her to send dinner for all of us tonight. There's the Laxes. Hi, Mr. and Mrs. Lax. Meet my friend, Paula. She'll be working the snowball stand this summer."

"Welcome to the Playground of Ohio, Paula. I hope you enjoy the work here," Mr. Lax encourages.

"I'm looking forward to it," she calls as she waves in passing.

Annie grabs Paula's arm and gives it a tug. "Don't be too friendly. Just enough. They'll know plenty about us in short order. ... Hi, Daddy. Give me the key and I'll show Paula how to open the snowball stand. "

At the stand Annie says, "This is your home away from both homes. It really takes two. Wait till I get the lock off the latch."

She lifts the hinged plywood door the width of the 8 x 10 stand and props it up with two 2 x 2 pieces of wood. Annie demonstrates the ice shaver that makes snow for the 5 flavors of syrup that gets added to the snow cones. Then the instructions for making cotton candy.

Annie flips on two switches. One starts the motor that turns the cylinder cup with holes in it and the other is the heat button. The cylinder sits in the middle of a great round aluminum pan with high sides. Annie instructs, "After it gets hot, maybe 3 or 4 minutes, you pour in a half cup of pink sugar. The heat melts the sugar and spins it out through the holes. The sides of the pan collect the spun sugar and you pick it up with the slender wand I showed you how to make last night at the house. When you aren't busy, you make up a lot of wands and grind a pile of ice. The size of the crowd and the heat of the day dictate the amount of ice and cotton candy you'll need. During the day kids buy more than adults do. You'll get the hang of it."

"I can't wait to get started. Let me try one," Paula begs.

"Wait a minute! I want to show you how the cash register works first and the order of how to close down the stand." Annie says in exasperation with Paula's impatient enthusiasm.

"Okay. Sorry"

"Every night around 9:30, Daddy will give you the high sign to close. You press the 'total key' and the 'drawer open' key. The register releases the paper that tells how much business was done for the day. Daddy has to pay the park manager a percentage of the take. The money and the paper go in a bag. Take the bag to Dad after you lower the front flap and lock up. Of course, you have to have the stand and the equipment cleaned and washed so it's ready to be used the next day. Don't forget to leave the key with Dad. In a few days you can learn about the French fry and corn dog stand because you'll have to relieve us for bathroom and lunch breaks on occasion. When you get used to it, you'll have a rhythm. It's easy."

"OK. Now can I make cotton candy?"

"Here's your apron. Cold running water is in the back sink. Go ahead, give it a try" Annie steps back making room for Paula.

The sugar spins nicely for a while then starts spitting hot melted sugar. It lands like sizzling, pelting rain on Paula's arms. "Ouch! Ouch! Ouch!"

"Here, turn the heat down. It got too hot." Annie moves back to let Paula in to the machine to try again.

The last try goes fine and in 10 minutes Paula is an expert.

"Can I make them ahead and put them in the holder?" Paula wants to know.

"Only if it's a dry day. If it's raining or humid, the cotton candy will melt and lose its form. You have to be the judge," Annie warns. "I gotta go help Dad now. Do you think you can manage it all right?"

"Yes. Look down from time to time and I'll wave OK or not," Paula urges her as Annie leaves Paula on her own.

The first hour was only slightly busy. The young boy from the Bus Station comes by. "I'm Davie. I heard you are working here this summer. Let me know if I can help. I love cotton and snow. I can run errands and deliver messages."

"OK. I'm Paula. I'll keep that in mind. ... Want to run an errand now?"

"Sure. For a little snow? Cherry?"

"OK, why not? Tell Mr. Harper I need change, OK?"

"Done." Davie bobs his head in the affirmative.

Rusty delivers five dollars in change and after Rusty leaves Davie comes around to collect his reward. Paula notices that Davie keeps his distance but shows up at the right time. He watches and listens. Smart little guy.

Paula gives him a half a snow cone with cherry syrup. She wants him to be her friend because he's a Gypsy boy. Paula is obsessed with knowing all the Gypsies.

"Do you think the ladies in the 'tea room' will read my palm?" Paula asks him.

"Don't know. I'll ask. ... How old are you?"

"Fourteen."

"You don't look fourteen, but I'll ask. ... Bye!"

Around 9:30 Rusty comes down to say it's time to clean up and close."I'll help lower the front so you can lock up," he says.

Paula washes the counter, wipes the syrup bottles clean, throws the left over ice in the lake behind the stand, and dries the tray. She washes the aluminum cotton candy pan, turns off the motor, the heat and then closes the register. All goes without problems.

Paula is surprised to see Chip. "Are you closing? I wanted to see what time you two get off so we can go pick up Breck."

Paula says, "I'm not sure but I think around 11:00. I'll be at the French fry stand helping clean up. We'll come down to Breck's. OK?"

Chip waves, "Yeah. We'll wait for you at the Pier."

The day was successful in every way. Paula is excited about having learned so much on her first day. She is disappointed though that it wasn't very busy.

When they get off, Mr. Harper instructs, "Take Rusty with you and don't be out too late."

After meeting up with the guys at the Pier they meander through the park for a while.

"What addition do we live in?" Paula asks Chip

"We all live in the Neel addition."

As the kids arrive at Harper's cottage, Annie invites the guys to sit on the porch while Rusty gets ready for bed.

The screened in porch has wicker furniture, bamboo blinds that roll up and down by way of a rope on each end. A glider sits across one end of the porch. Two floor lamps and a radio make it quite a comfortable place to entertain and be sufficiently visible when boys are present.

Inside the cottage is basic furniture. The living room contains a daybed, rocking chair, a couple of folding chairs and a wicker couch with kay-pock cushions and the sixth dining chair. When renters have weekend guests they can sleep the most people in a small space. "Got any cards? We can play rummy." Breck calls as he lowers the blinds on the sides of the porch, pulls up two chairs and scoots a table in front of the glider. Paula gets out cards and hands pencil and paper to Chip. They score to 300 by the time Rusty finishes his bubble bath and shows up in his P.J.'s

Annie says, "We'd better sign off now. Rusty will want a snack. He's likely to become the boss's secretary when the flow doesn't include him."

"Can we walk you home tomorrow night?" Breck asks as they head out the screen door.

"Sure. About the same time, I guess. Night! See you."
The girls agree. As advertised, Rusty says, "I'm hungry."

"Do you want a peanut butter sandwich? We'll have more to offer after we go to the store," Annie tells him.

" ...if I can have some milk with it."

\* \* \*

After fixing his snack Paula heads for the tub for her turn with the bubble bath. Airing out did the trick. The musty odor is gone. The only smells now are of Breck shampoo, White Shoulders cologne, and Beechnut gum. Paula's "Mom" gave her recipe for making rooms smell nice. You chew the gum till it's just soft enough to roll in your palms but not stick to your skin. Place a couple balls in a clean ashtray because you might want to chew the gum later if you run out. Soon the room smells like mint gum.

A four drawer dresser (two drawers for each girl), stands next to the hall tree for sweaters and jackets at the top of the stairs. Two hooks are mounted on the wall for their robes and pajamas. Pictures of Niagara Falls and the famous Dionne quintuplets like the ones that hang in Maw Emmy's house on the farm date the decorating but all the same gives their private space a cozy feeling. Paula has never felt like she had a private space. She smiles and says "How about this, Leonard?"

Annie tucks Rusty in to bed and says, "Daddy will be home soon. I'm going upstairs now. If you want anything, just call loud enough." She kisses his forehead and gives him a short wave then joins Paula.

"Were you surprised when Chip showed up tonight?" Annie grins ear to ear.

Paula put her hands over her face and gave a mild scream. "Not only that but I thought your dad might not like it so soon in the acquaintance. I was holding my breath for a lecture."

"Daddy knows I met them earlier so he didn't give it a second thought. Now, he might have said something if we had not taken Rusty with us. You are handling things just right. Not being too forward and letting Daddy lead the progress. You will soon feel at home with him. You'll see. .... It must be hard though."

Paula shakes her head "yes... and ... they want to pick us up again tonight. Is this going to be a nightly happening? Are you all right with it?"

"You must be kidding! Does it sound like I'm crying?" Annie hugs her pillow.

After a short silence Annie says, "We have to go see the court lady soon. She wants to talk to us all." She reaches up, turns out the light and says "good night. See you in the morning." to Paula who is already asleep.

Next morning Paula resumes her habit of starting each day by writing in her diary.

Dear Diary, Tuesday, June 7, 1949
        Mr. Harper says to be ready to leave by 9:30. That will get us to Columbus for an 11:00 appointment. Mrs. Clark wants to interview Annie AND me.
        I don't know why Mrs. Clark wants to talk to me. I don't have anything to do with the divorce. We'll go to the store for groceries on the way back. I never realized that my class in home ec would be put to use so soon. Bye for now.            P.B.

* * *

The car is hot. Rusty asks his dad, "Will we get to see Mother while we're in Columbus?"

"Not today. We have to wait for the judge's decision on where and how often. Time will pass quickly," Mr. Harper tells his son.

57

Rusty is heartbroken. When tears slide down his cheek, Paula hands him the hanky from her pocket. Mr. Harper parks on Fulton Street and has time to spare. Paula checks her watch and hopes she will be first to see Mrs. Clark.

Upon arrival at the counselor's office, Mrs. Clark greets them. "Welcome! How was traffic coming in from the Lake?"

"Not bad. We left after the morning workday traffic died down," Mr. Harper tells her.

"Let's see. Which one of you is Annie's friend, Paula? The young lady with the dark hair has brown eyes like I'm assuming her brother. So, the blue eyed lass must be Paula, right?"

Mr. Harper says, "Good assumption. These are my two, Annie and Rusty."

"Have a seat, children. Paula, if you'll come with me, please. We'll have a little chat and then I'll talk to Annie and Rusty. We should be finished in about forty-five minutes."

Paula enters Mrs. Clark's spacious office. She notices some interesting toys on a long table: a doll house and stacks of colored paper, crayons, some picture books and a couple of dolls.

"Have a seat, Paula. If you're wondering about the toys, they are for assisting in communication with different aged children. Some are afraid to talk or are too angry to talk. Sometimes, I just watch them play for a while. It gives me some clues for approaching the child. Do you need a toy?"

Paula smiles. "No thanks. I don't have any trouble talking. Ask my homeroom teacher."

"I see you have a sense of humor. That's a good thing. The reason I want to talk to you is that I have to make a decision about whether the children will live with their father or not. If they do, I have to decide how often and under what circumstances they get to visit their mother. I'm looking to you for some insight. Would you be willing to help me out?"

58

"Sure. I'm happy to help. Annie seems a little nervous about the outcome of the meeting today. She misses her mother, but she really wants to be at the lake with her dad."

"That's what I wanted to hear. How do you two get along? I understand you are school friends."

"Yes. We met on the city bus. She saw me holding a *Latin I* book on my lap. She recognized it as the same book used at our school and starts talking to me. We both play the piano and neither of us knew anyone else at school. So, we got together to play duets."

"How did your parents come to allow you to spend the summer with Mr. Harper?"

"My grandparents on the farm are ill and need help. My parents planned to spend the summer with them and make further decisions when school is about to start in September. Mr. Harper asked Annie and me if we wanted to spend the summer together. What do YOU think? Seeing how enthusiastic we were about the idea, he approached my mother with the plan. Mr. Harper is letting me work for him like Annie does. We are getting along really well."

"Don't you miss your parents?"

"It's been only two days. Even if I was with them, I wouldn't be home. I'd rather be at the lake and not home than on the farm and not home. Annie and I are like sisters. Rusty is a neat kid. He spends most of the time shadowing his dad."

"Tell me how your day goes, Paula."

"So far the plan is this. We get up about 8:00 or so. We'll have breakfast on our own. Whatever we want – cereal or eggs. One day a week Annie and I will do laundry. Monday seems to be the best day. We go to work between ten and eleven. We'll eat lunch at work. Mr. Harper plans to take Rusty to work with him. Today we will go to the store before we go home. We have a list of food we want to have at the house so we can cook if we feel like it. Much of how our day goes will depend on the weather and the crowd.

Annie and I have talked endlessly about the priorities. I was introduced to my job at the snowball stand yesterday. ... I love it. It seems more like play than work. Annie will work with her dad and Rusty not far away and in plain view if I need anything or if they need me to relieve one of them."

"Do you have any play time? You know, like socializing with other kids?"

"Sure! All the kids our age who live at the lake either have jobs at the park or babysit younger brothers and sisters, so the parents can work. We will usually get off between 9:30 or 10:00. We then can meet up with some of the other kids."

"What can you do that late at night?"

"We can go roller skating, watch the late Free Act, go to the Crystal Ballroom to dance, or go on some rides. Things like that. It IS an amusement park. Sometimes we might want to play miniature golf. We might just walk around and say 'Hi' to other kids who are still working. One of our friends, J2, is Bozo when his brother, Moose, isn't. We throw the ball and dunk him. He draws a crowd. It wears him out good. Sometimes, he wants us to go away. We can really just do whatever we feel like doing when we get off work. There isn't time to be bored." Paula is careful not to mention Chip and Breck.

"What time do you go home?" Mrs. Clark asks

"Usually about 11:30. We always check with Annie's dad so he knows what we're doing and when we're going home. It seems to work so far. I go to Mass on Sunday and sometimes Annie goes with me."

"Do you think Annie and Rusty would prefer living with their mother?"

"I don't think they'd like to choose. They seem satisfied with the routine at the Lake. Annie and I take Rusty with us sometimes, but mostly he stays with his dad."

"Paula, you've been very helpful."

Mr. Harper is last to see Mrs. Clark. She says, "Of course what I say at this time is just a recommendation, Mr. Harper. I feel confident that things are running smoothly. The judge can override my decision if he disagrees. If any of you, including Paula, ever want to talk to me about anything that is troubling you, just call for an appointment. You will get top priority to meet with me. This goes for any difficulties you have concerning your family or Paula's. Your idea to invite her to stay with you was an excellent one for Annie. Is that OK with you?"

"Yes, more than all right, Mrs. Clark. It's nice to know there's someone to guide us all if we need advice. Paula also knows the priest. He knows her family. Sometimes that's a good thing, but sometimes not," he chuckles.

Mrs. Clark nods in agreement. She knows what Mr. Harper means.

Mrs. Clark puts her arms on Annie's and Rusty's shoulders while walking them to the exit door of the waiting room.

Mr. Harper wants to know all the details of their conversations. Everyone is glad it's over. Paula assures him that life at the lake is working well. Rusty busies himself with two new Captain Marvel and Superman comic books.

Annie wants to know where the nearest A & P supermarket is." I know how to fix creamed peas and potatoes," she offers.

Paula adds, "I like pork chops and I'll make a big salad. I'll bet Rusty likes corn. That's one good meal."

Annie says. "Let's see how one big meal goes before we stock up. The refrigerator is small and we'll need to eat the meat soon while it's fresh."

Paula retorts, "Good thinking. Keep reminding me of those little details. ... I'm fussy about the laundry. Is Rinso soap, Satina starch, and Clorox ok with you? You choose next time."

Annie agrees and adds, "Dad will want a bar of Lifeboy for home and Lava soap for the stand. ... What kind of cereal do you want Rusty?"

"Wheaties with Jack Armstrong on the box," he says.

Dad adds, "two quarts of milk, Folgers coffee, cream, sugar, four cans of Campbell's soup (we have some chilly days), soda crackers and a dozen eggs."

Rusty says, "Don't forget the Wonder bread if that's the one with the polka dots. Band-aids, mercurochrome for Paula when she forgets to take her hand out of the ice shaver."

Rusty was the only one laughing at his joke.

Everyone is more relaxed on the way home than when they drove to Columbus.

Next day, Mr. Harper says, "OK Paula, Annie can open the snowball stand today and you can learn the French fry and corn dog business."

"Yeah! Now I really feel like part of the team."

After opening the stand, Mr. Harper begins his instruction.

"First thing is to load up the potato peeler with potatoes, see? It looks like a cement mixer. When the motor is turned on, the potatoes are thrown against the side wall which wears off the skin. When the tumbler stops, you check to see if any potato eyes need removed. That's done by hand."

"Step three, you put a potato in the slicer. See how the potato fits right in there? Pull the lever and the potato is shoved through the 4 x 4 cross cut blades. There you have your potato strips. They are put into a tub of cold water to soak. As you need them, you load them into a French fry basket and shake to remove water drops. They go in a fryer for blanching then mount the basket on the back over the fryer for the oil to drain off. Monitor carefully to be sure there are always blanched fries ready for browning when the customers place an order. Serve the French fries in two sizes of paper cups. Any questions?"

"No. I think I have it," as Paula nods.

"OK! Now, for the corn dogs. We keep a tray of hot dogs on skewers ready at all times. Be sure there is always batter made and in the refrigerator. Always wear a clean apron. Hold the hot dog by the stick, dip the hot dog in the batter, give it a twist, place in the hot oil and mount the stick on the clip." He demonstrates the wrist movement. "Fry until lightly browned. More customers want the outside painted with mustard than not. They will tell you. Wrap the stick in a napkin and lay it in the scalloped paper tray. Now feed the overall instructions back to me."

Paula repeats the processes, emphasizing "Make sure there are always blanched potatoes ready for the frying oil and there are skewered dogs and batter ready for the corn dog oil. Got it. How about clean up?"

"It's a joint effort. You'll never have to do it alone. I'll give instructions as we go."

Dear Diary, Thursday June 9, 1949:

"The first day in the French fry stand went well, but I'll be glad to return to the snowball stand tomorrow.

I saw Breck's dad walking with Debby Jackson and Breck this afternoon. Breck acted like he didn't know me. He didn't speak or anything. Odd! They looked like they had been out in the Chris Craft. Mr. Dempsy had on his skipper cap and all of them wore sneakers and windbreakers. I wonder what that was all about. Breck said at the Bus Station that Debby wasn't his girlfriend anymore. You sure wouldn't have known it by the looks of them this afternoon. I wonder if he's sore about something. I'll ask Chip if he knows.  Later, PB

# PATTE BURGOON

# CHAPTER VII
## BLUE GOOSE

Dear Diary, Monday, June 13, 1949

It is such a great feeling to look forward to waking up every day. That is new and different for me. Annie and I have a lot of work to do that our mothers used to do for us: Laundry and cooking some meals, ironing, keeping track of supplies around the house. We have enough fun to make up for our having to do it all. Her dad keeps his sense of humor most of the time.

Annie's birthday is this week. She turns 14. I think her mother is coming in from Columbus with a cake. Maybe she'll cook dinner too. Anyway, I want to do something special for Annie. I'll work for her so she can have time off. *Leonard seems happy all the time too.*

It's been really hot. Maybe we can go swimming today.

Later, P.B.


"Annie, Rusty, you want pancakes for breakfast?" Paula calls out.

"Sounds good," Rusty answers from the bathroom. "Got any Kayro with the green label?"

"Sorry, no. What's the green label got to do with it?"

"It's got maple flavoring now."

Paula groans, "Jeezus! ... We'll get some next time."

Rusty looks down at his plate and says rather sheepishly," I think Daddy has a girlfriend."

"What makes you think so? You are always inventing stuff," Annie accuses.

"I heard him talking to Mr. McElroy yesterday. Daddy said there was a sweet little waitress at Clay's restaurant across from Star Boats. Then he said some more, but his voice went quiet like a whisper. Then I heard them laughing."

"Was the potato peeler running? Maybe Dad was telling Mr. McElroy a joke." Annie continues frying eggs.

Rusty mutters as he pours the last of the dark Kayro syrup with the blue label on his pancake, "I still think daddy's got a girlfriend."

Paula asks Annie, "Do you think we can go swimming today? Would your dad let us off a couple hours after we get the stands open? We aren't that busy on Mondays are we?"

"He probably will. This might be the last chance we can ask for time off until after the 4th. People are getting ready for their holiday company. The weekend of the 4th you won't be able to catch your breath. Folks will be lined up buying fries, dogs, drinks. It's supposed to be hot. You'll be busy, too. You won't be able to stir 'em with a stick."

Rusty laughs so hard he starts to choke. "Can you just see some big giant stirring the people with a stick and scraping them into a giant pot for stew?" He continues laughing.

Annie points her finger at him, "You read too many funny books. It's affecting your personality. Rinse your plate and get ready to go to the park." She muses up his hair. Rusty's growing tall she notices. His voice is changing also.

While quickly washing their dishes, Annie whispers to Paula, "Got any Kotex? I meant to put it on the grocery list but forgot. Sorry."

"There's one in my train case and one more in the box."

"Got any Midol?"

"I don't use it. Aren't you early?" Paula asks.

"I'm due tomorrow. I just don't want to be caught without sanitary napkins when we start getting busy for the weekend." Annie explains.

"Good thinking. We can pick up some tomorrow," Paula says as she grabs the beach towels, bathing suits and a dollar from her cigar box. "Let's scoot. Come on, Rusty."

He reminds her, "Don't forget the green label."

"I'll slap a green label on you." Paula warns him as he ducks her swipe at him.

At the stand, Annie corners her dad. "We haven't gotten to go swimming yet and the 4th of July will be here before you know it. Can we take some time later this afternoon, Daddy?"

Mr. Harper says, "Good idea. I'm going to break-in Jessie Connor to work the snowball stand. She can work with you today, Paula. That way, we'll have extra help on the 4th. Then Paula can help out here or there, wherever is the busiest. How about 2:30 to 4:30? Want to take Rusty?"

"Does a chicken have lips?" Annie murmers.

"OK, Smarty Pants. Oh! I forgot to tell you. Your mother won't be able to make it for your birthday. Maybe next week. And, Rusty needs some fun too. I'll go round up Jessie and get her over here. She can give you girls more time off for some daytime fun."

"Thanks, Daddy. Rusty CAN come too."

Paula notices the disappointment on Annie's face when her dad just glances over the fact that her mother isn't coming to the next item, without even taking a breath. She moves over beside Annie and gives her a squeeze in acknowledgement of the slight.

Paula left for the snowball stand. She had just finished shaving the ice when Mr. Harper brings Jessie.

"Hi, Jessie. Ready to learn the tricks of the trade?"

"Yeah, I guess so."

"Don't be too enthusiastic. You might enjoy it," Paula says as she tosses Jessie an apron. "I'll bet your mom's glad you are getting a job."

Mr. Harper waves "Bye" and heads back to the French fry stand.

Paula turns out to be a good teacher. She tells Jessie, "The important thing is to keep your eye on the supplies, the crowd and the weather. Don't have too much made up if the weather is bad and don't let yourself run out if the crowd is heavy. When you aren't busy, make the skinny wands to hold the cotton candy. Can't have too many of them."

When Jessie has trouble with the cotton candy wands, Paula urges, "Keep trying. You'll get the hang of it."

Finally, on number seven, Jessie figures out what she's doing wrong and she goes full speed ahead.

On his way to the fun house, J1 shouts to Paula "I'm going to open up for my aunt today."

"Annie and I are going swimming today. Want to go?"

"Sounds good. OK if I bring J2?"

"Of course! Pass the word. See if Breck and Chip want to go."

"I'll ask Breck. I saw him at the drug store a bit ago. He can ask Chip. I'll get back to you."

Davie shows up. "I need some cotton."

"Are you working for me?" Paula asks.

"Yeah! I got a message. I need some cotton."

"Jessie, Davie is my guy. I keep him in half orders of cotton and ice and he keeps me in half orders of information. He's like the Indian that reads the smoke signals."

Jessie laughs. She finishes twirling the cotton. "By the way, speaking of smoke signals, have you seen the Cherokee Chief, Big John, lately?"

Davie says, "I always see the Chief. Me and him is good buddies. He's gonna train me to be a Shaman." Davie takes the cotton candy and gives forth with the news. "Breck can't go. Chip doesn't want to go. J2 will catch up with you. J1 doesn't have money for the pool. I need ice."

Paula makes him half a snow cone. "Take a breath. Cherry?"

"Lime."

She hands it to him. Paula says, "… and?"

"And J1 knows someone on the Little Lake that will be gone this afternoon and gave permission to use their dock to swim off of."

"OK, Davie, you did good. You think you'll be alright here by yourself, Jessie?"

"Yeah." She continues making cotton candy wands.

Annie, Rusty and Paula hook up with J1 and J2 at the willow tree on the park side of the bridge that crosses to Picnic Point. Rusty borrows an inner tube from the guy, who has the grocery wheel next to the French fry stand, and then runs home for a bath towel. "Never know when you'll need a little baby oil," Paula tells Annie. "I've got some in my bag."

J1 points to the third dock up, where a motor boat is hoisted out of the water. "That's where we'll swim."

"Are you sure it's OK?" asks Annie.

Rusty wants to know, "How deep?"

"Over your head so no horsing around." Annie places a light grip on Rusty's shoulder.

"I got '*per-me-shan*.' J1 tells them as they spread their towels. "They are going to Newark for the day. ... shopping for their holiday company. They are friends of my aunts."

"Where's your suit?" Rusty asks as Annie slathers him with oil.

"Don't need a suit," says J2. "Moose, is wearing OUR suit at the Bozo site. I get it tonight. Cut-off jeans will be fine."

Paula oils Annie and finishes her own legs when J2 calls to J1, "Go ya to the dips."

J2 dives in followed by J1 and Paula calls "Hey, wait for me!" In she goes. They don't wait for anybody.

* * *

Annie helps Rusty with the inner tube. She is not competitive. She dangles her feet off the edge of the dock. The water is still a little on the cool side, but she doesn't really care because she doesn't plan to go in above the ankle.

Paula is about 50 feet behind the guys who reach the dips and are on their way back. "I don't think I'm going to make it," she pants.

One of them says, "Sure you can." They keep churning water as fast as they can.

They continue their race while Paula starts to panic. She struggles to keep going. She tries to stand up, but the water is too deep. "Something is touching my feet!" She screams, and then she starts talking to Leonard who answers, *"Old girl,"* he says, *"you'd better float on your back and rest. Nobody is going to help you. Just relax and head back to the dock. You don't need to make it to the dips." Leonard, also on the verge of panic, starts to settle down.* Paula's heart beat slows and she does a side stroke. She finally reaches the dock and just hangs on to the steps for a while. "I am glad I made it. You guys have no idea how scared I was."

J2 says, "Gee, Paula. I thought you were kidding. "

J1 agrees, "No hard feelings?"

Paula shrugs, "I guess I had no business trying to go that far. I had no idea you guys were so serious about your challenges. That puts a different spin on the race at the Bus Station. Next time I hear, 'Go ya' ... I'll get the heck out of the way."

All but Rusty are finally on the dock.

J1 says to Annie, "You ain't even wet yet," as he shoves her over the side of the dock.

The dock shakes with laughter. Annie is a good sport about it. She hauls Rusty to the dock and the guys help her get him out of the tube and on to the warm wooden surface. They help Annie out of the lake. It's now time to head back to their waiting jobs.

* * *

The guys take Rusty to the public rest room below the Crystal Ballroom to put on dry clothes. J2 just let his jeans air dry.

That night Chip comes by at closing time. He helps Paula with the routine closing. They pick up Annie as usual and head to Playland Pier to pick up Breck. Paula tells Chip about seeing Breck with Debby.

Chip explains, "It's been a long standing promise his dad made to Debby. Mr. Dempsy couldn't very well take Debby without Breck, if you know what I mean."

"That makes sense then." Paula is satisfied with the story.

On the way out of the park, Breck says, "Sorry I couldn't go swimming. I had to cut the grass. But, I made a deal with Dad for next Tuesday. He said I can have the Chris Craft for two hours. When he says two hours, he means an hour and fifty-nine. So! You two want to go?"

"What time is on your schedule?" Annie asks.

"Chip and I will go out at nine. We'll pick you up on the far side of Picnic Point at 10:00. You can't tell anyone because Chip is the only one allowed in the boat with me."

"All right!" Paula squeals.

"OK – Chris Craft on Tuesday," Annie agrees.

* * *

The heat is moving in. It is so hot in their half story bedroom that the girls haven't been able to sleep very well.

"Daddy, please can we move our bed to the screened-in porch?" Annie pleads.

"If we are quiet and lights out by 11:30 no one will know we are there," Paula adds.

After some exploration of the pros and cons, Mr. Harper says, "If you promise not to broadcast you are there, you can try it out for one week. If it doesn't work, back upstairs you go and I don't care how hot it is."

Dear Diary, Wednesday, June 15, 1949 Annie's birthday.

We moved furniture around yesterday to accommodate a daybed that opens up to sleep two. I gave Annie a friendship ring for her birthday. We had a good night's sleep finally. Whatever breeze there was to be had, we got it.

Later, P.B.

On Saturday night, June 18, the girls work until 12:30. "Where do you think Breck and Chip are tonight?" Paula asks Annie.

"It seems like everybody's schedule is messed up because of the coming holiday." She figures.

"Wouldn't you think one of them would have stopped by to let us know what they're doing?" Paula yawns. Annie is already asleep and Paula is quick to follow.

Sometime later, outside the screen door are some whispers. "Psst! Paula!"

"What? Who's out there?" Paula sits up on her elbows.

"It's Chip. Wake up."

"What do you want? God! What time is it?"

Breck whispers as loud as he dares, "Wake up, Annie."

She rallies, "What's going on?"

"Breck and Chip are outside." Paula tells her.

"What do they want? God! What time is it?" She asks as she reaches for the flashlight she keeps by the bed. "Geez, you guys! It's 2:15. What's going on?"

"Throw on some clothes and come with us," Breck says. "We're going to Blue Goose."

Paula asks, "What's Blue Goose? Where's Blue Goose?"

"We've been fishing. Nothing is biting. We rented a row boat at Blue Goose," Chip whispers. "So, we have to return it."

"I can't believe you guys."

"Come on! Go with us. It'll be fun," Chip whispers more urgently. "Come on! We have to return the boat."

"How do we get back?" Annie wants to know.

"Shank's mare." You know! Walk! Come on. Help us row," they beg.

Paula wants more details, "Now wait a minute. How much crap do you have in the boat?"

"Don't worry, 'Paula, the thorough.' Just a couple flashlights. We already dropped off the tackle, cooler, and poles at my house," Breck says, trying to put an end to the questions and objections.

"It's Sunday. I have to go to mass."

"You'll be back in time. I promise," adds Chip.

"Do you want to go with those jerks?" Annie asks in disbelief. "Will we be back by daylight?"

"If you hurry up we will. If not, we won't. Come on," Breck pleads.

Annie zips up her shorts and roots around for our canvas shoes and socks under the bed.

"I guess we're going," Paula says. "Go by the garage in the shadows. I don't want anyone seeing us out this late."

"OK, hurry!"

Paula quickly gets dressed. "You got my right shoe. Here's yours."

They slip out the screen door. Luckily the screen snap latch makes no noise. The four head down Second Street to Third. They cross over the highway to reduce chances of being seen.

"I can't believe we're doing this," Paula groans. "I can't put this in my diary."

"Me neither," adds Annie.

They maneuver around until they are in their usual pairs. "Where's the boat?"

"Tied up at the end of the Playland Pier," answers Chip.

Only a few lights here and there shine in the park. The Bus Station and the Pinkie are both dark. It's 2:30 a.m. Williams Restaurant is dimly lit, but quiet. No traffic. Everything closes down by 1:00 at the park and the staff and drunks are gone by 2:00 usually. So they say!

At the end of the pier Breck reaches out his hand to Annie. "Let me help steady you so you don't fall in. Chip, get in first and help keep the boat firm against the pier."

Paula muses to herself and Leonard, "I am really enjoying the adventure. We wouldn't have come if we didn't know them so well by now." She senses Leonard's approval too.

Chip says, "I'll take the oars first and get us to the middle of the lake." At Picnic Point he offers the oars to Paula. "Want to row?"

"Sure, I'll take a turn. I like to row but I'm not very good at it."

"You'll be a pro by the time we get to Blue Goose."

"How far is it anyway?"

"Oh, a couple of city blocks or so," he says.

Annie whines, "You guys sit still. With all the seat changing I'll be swimming. I don't know why I agreed to this. I hate boats."

Chip asks, "You two CAN swim, can't you?"

"Yes. We'll be OK," Paula keeps rowing. "You told us nothing was biting. Does that include the mosquitoes or aren't they big enough to keep? It's hard to swat while rowing - SHIT! - I can't stand this!" Paula continues to flail around and row.

Chip grabs the light. "Those are only gnats. 'Girls will be girls.'"

Breck grabs the light from Chip. "Those are elephants if I ever saw one. Did you bring the shot gun, Chip?"

They try to restrain laughing. They don't want to draw attention to the four in the boat.

"Assholes!" Paula says half under her breath.

"Oops! There goes the sin budget," Annie is quick to notice.

Breck finally settles them down and offers to take the oars.

"Watch out! Don't tip the boat completely over," he directs.

"Why, no matter how good a row boat, is there always at least an inch of water in the bottom? My shoes and socks are soaked," complains Paula.

"Quit groaning. That's just how it is when you go fishing, Paula. I'll have to take you out and educate you." Chip adds.

"Oh! You promise? I can't wait."

"Keep your voices down, you guys. Sound magnifies across the water," Breck whispers as he continues rowing.

Annie says, "You are making more progress than she did. How soon will we be there?"

"That sounds like my little brother when we are taking a ride, 'How soon we gonna be there, Daddy?'" Breck mocks little Collie. "You girls are turning out to be a pain."

Chip murmurs in Paula's ear, "A nice pain though." As he squeezes her hand. Paula is surprised. *That's the only time he has touched me. I wonder if he'll ever get around to kissing me!*

Swoosh! . . . Swoosh! . . . The oars keep rhythmically breaking the surface of the water.

"What the . . ." Paula ducks and puts her head in the crook of her arm.

Annie screams, "What was that?"

"Must have been an eagle," Breck says. "Or a condor, maybe."

Chip corrects Breck, "Don't worry. They're just bats."

"Just bats? I heard if you get one caught in your hair you have to have your hair shaved off." Paula is near panic. (Leonard's head is under her arm. Her head is under Chip's arm.)

Breck quietly urges again, "Shh! ... Be quiet. ... You can practically hear whispers across the lake. They must be playing poker. Some guy just said he folded."

"I'd ask why sound travels so loud across water but I'm not in the mood for another 'dog and pony show.'"

The night is dead quiet except for the sound of the squeaking oars where the pins fit into the metal lined holes along the sides of the boat.

Just then another bat swoops down toward Paula. She takes a quick trip over the side of the boat into the water. "Holy shit! You guys didn't highlight the hazards. Couldn't you have taken the boat back in daylight?" She dog- paddles close to the side of the boat.

They are laughing their butts off at Paula's reaction to the bats. Annie gets mad and shoves Chip over the side. He grabs for her and she, too, is in the drink.

"We wanted your help rowing and your lovely company walking back. What were we thinking?" mutters Breck.

Paula is hanging on to the rear of the boat while still dog paddling. "Damn it! Something just touched my feet!" She screams as softly as she can, but panicky. "Help me back in the boat. I can't stand touching anything in the lake. Hurry! Eek! There it is again!" As Breck tries to help her in, Chip climbs back in and rocks the boat far enough that Breck loses his balance. In he goes. "Shh! Shh! Shh! Blub! Blub! Maybe bringing you two wasn't such a good idea."

As they all get back in the rowboat, the two guys and Paula are dying laughing, but Annie is sobbing. Chip is rowing. After all - especially Annie - are settled down, Breck puts his arm around her. All is calm finally.

"So much for the 'return boat' expedition," Paula mutters. "What was touching me in the water, a 40 pound catfish?"

"No," Breck tells her. "Probably a floating island." He scans the water's surface and spots a flag on a stick standing straight up out of the water.

"Oh, you are SUCH A LIAR," Paula accuses.

"No. Seriously," Chip adds, "That's one of the jobs of the Lake Patrol. Large masses of sphagnum moss let loose from the bottom of the lake. They float beneath the water's surface. Thus, 'floating islands.' They put a flag on them so motor boats don't run into them and ruin their rudders."

"One lies and the other one swears to it. I never know when to believe you guys," Annie said, only half believing.

They rowed about a mile by water which was Breck's guess. It felt like two miles. They saw two fishermen in a boat with a lantern. A blue light shone at the end of a pier. "Ah! Blue Goose. All we have to do is row the boat on to the grassy beach far enough so we can get out." Breck said with a sigh of relief.

"We're wet soggy messes. Oops! No working wrist watch ... the sun is coming up. I'd say it is pretty but I'm getting anxious and not in any mood to hear or appreciate any of your stories right now," Paula complains.

Chip leads the way through empty lots, fields, gravel driveways, barking dogs, over fences, through addition after addition, all the while dodging the Sunday paper carrier.

They keep up a serious pace, until they reach Picnic Point where they stop to rest at a table. Chip asks Paula, "Are you OK?"

"I hope when I'm old I can look back on tonight and laugh. At least my clothes are dry." She feels the bottom of her shorts and shirt.

They see the guy drop off bundled newspapers at the Bus Station. "Let's weave in and out of streets where we don't know anybody," Annie shrinks back so as not to be seen.

"I don't think anybody saw us." Breck insists.

He and Chip wave goodbye and make their way home after they drop off the girls.

As the girls slip under the covers, Annie says, "Put your pj's back on in case Daddy gets up before 8:00." Finally both start to laugh.

"I've got blisters on my hands. There are scratches on my legs and no curl in my hair. We've got a half hour before we have to get up and get ready for church. I can't believe we did this," quietly moans Paula.

"Good thing we laid out our clothes before going to bed," said Annie, "But I'll have to wear my sandals. What a night!"

Mr. Harper is having coffee when they get up. He comments, "You girls look like you had a rough night."

Paula blushes while turning away from his gaze. After Mass they go to work at the stands as usual.

A couple hours after mass Annie relieves Paula for a bathroom break. "Did you see Breck?"

"No. Why?"

"He has pink calamine lotion on his neck and arms."

"So…what's that for?"

"Poison ivy. He really has a bad dose of it," she grins.

"Oh no! Do you suppose that's what I have on my legs? They itch like crazy." Paula lifts her skirt to show Annie.

"Yep! You got it too."

Fortunately no one notices that both Breck AND Paula have poison ivy. Paula steers clear of his house.

Paula tells Mr. Harper, "There is something called 'Ivy Dry' in the medicine cabinet. Is that as good as calamine lotion for poison ivy? I can't figure out where I picked this up." *One more offense against my sin budget.*

Annie puts her hand over her mouth to hide her grin.

He shakes his head "Yes" and gives her a "Tch! Tch!"

All Annie has to do is motion toward her sore hands. "I can't believe we did that."

\* \* \*

They both laugh and the secret keeps them entertained all of Sunday and Monday.

Monday night the guys come by. They have grins a mile wide on their faces.

"I don't want to hear about it. I have poison ivy, too," groans Paula.

They all roar laughing.

Breck says," I just want to confirm Tuesday plans. I was afraid you'd change your mind after Saturday night."

## CHAPTER VIII
## THE BOAT HOUSE

"Yeah," Annie told Breck. "We'll be at Picnic Point from 10:00 Tuesday morning until 10:55. Is that about right?"

Paula interrupts, "Is 55 minutes in a Chris Craft going to make up for Blue Goose and poison ivy?"

"No, better think 10:00 to 10:45 to give Chip and me time to dock the boat. I have a worse case of poison ivy than you do, Paula, and yes, it was worth it."

Monday night the guys pick up the girls. It had become a nightly ritual for Breck, Annie, Chip and Paula. They are basically shy teenagers basking in emotion. Even though, their feelings for each other go unspoken. They do their usual horsing around while looking forward to the boat ride the next morning.

When J1 joins them, Chip asks, as usual, "Where's J2?"

"Doing his Bozo thing relieving Moose."

J1 gives his version of the swimming escapades in Little Lake while laughing at the girls. "Paula couldn't keep up and Annie didn't even try." He put his arm around Breck to join him in song, *"We are the joy boys of radio: Hello, Hello, Hello-o-o-"*

However, Chip and Breck don't share the adventure they just had with the girls.

Breck sings, *"Life is like a mountain railroad, with an engineer that's brave."* with J1 who harmonizes, *"You must make the run successful from the cradle to the grave. Watch the curves that fill the tunnel. Never falter, never fail . . . "*

\* \* \*

While they're climbing a hill by the Lake Breeze Hotel, Chip reaches a hand out to Paula. When she reaches the top, he doesn't let go of her hand.

*Well, that's two*, she thought.

*Leonard agrees, if she is remembering Chip's attention in the boat.*

Paula is overcome with emotion. She can't get Leonard to quiet himself either. Her heart races and she feels tingly in the pit of her stomach.

Breck and J1 continue singing as they reach the top of the hill . . . *"Keep your hands upon the throttle and your eyes upon the rail. Blessed Savior . . .*

Trying to climb through a fence, Paula bangs her head. "Ow! Ow!" She reaches her hand up to rub her head.

Chip pulls her close to him and says, "Where does it hurt? Poor baby." He kisses it to make it better. "OK?"

"That's much better." she feels like purring. The wall of separation between Paula and Chip comes tumbling down and lands in a puddle of "shy." These feelings are a new experience for Paula, who isn't about to make any corrections. She is weak in the knees and just wants to be in his arms, hands? She doesn't much care which.

Paula has lost sight of Annie but hears the guys continue singing, *". . . till we reach that blissful shore – and the angels wait to join us . . ."*

\* \* \*

By the time they reach the Harper's cottage, Chip is comfortable enough to kiss Paula good night on the lips. "See you at 10:00."

"Nine fifty-five," Paula says as she squeezes his hand.

The guys leave. The girls go to their bedroom to dress for bed.

82

Annie nudges Paula, "Well, tell all. I saw that kiss Chip planted on you."

Paula tells her about his touch in the rowboat. "Tonight he kissed my head after I bumped it on a fence slat. When that didn't kill him he risked kissing me 'goodnight.' That's where we are."

Annie finished pin-curling her hair. "Man-o-man! When one little thing happens it's like a row of standing dominoes come tumbling down."

After putting on their pj's they return to the front porch. Paula continues, "Yes! I was beginning to wonder if he would ever kiss me. Now, I'm wondering how far it is going to go. Can we ever get it to where we want it and just keep it there?"

Getting no answer from Annie, she sighed and turned out the light.

* * *

Mr. Harper and Rusty leave for Newark about 9:15 the next morning to run some errands. Annie and Paula hurry through their morning routine. Bed made. Dishes done. They plan everything like clockwork because they have to open the stands by themselves at 11:15. By 9:55 the girls are at the far side of Picnic Point as directed, with canvas shoes in hand. They wade to the boat, being careful not to fall. Chip and Breck help them into the boat. Annie sits in front with Breck and Paula gets in the back with Chip.

The emotions from last night are still fresh. Chip puts his arm around Paula. "My hair is caught in my locket," she says as the boat pulls out heading for the center of the lake. "Ooh – ouch - -ouch." Chip tries to help get her long hair loose. More touching. They are getting more and more comfortable with each other.

"Where to?" Breck calls.

"Ice cream at Weldon's in Millersport," Chip says.

"Millersport, Ho!" cries Breck as he guns the motor.

The sun breaks through the filtering clouds. Chip and Paula receive an occasional spray when Breck and a couple other smart aleck boaters cross wakes and Breck has to make some fast maneuvers.

Chip calls out, "If you want to take the boat out again, you'd better settle down. Not that I mind a lap full of girl."

"Yeah! Yeah!" says Breck from the front. However, he complies with the warning reminder.

"Where'd you get the locket? I didn't notice you wearing it before," Chip asks Paula as he straightens it around her neck.

"I usually wear it, but it gets tucked in my shirt most of the time. There's a picture of me on one side and Maw Emma Bradley on the other. She's also my godmother."

"That's nice," he says as he kisses her neck. Paula shivers at the touch of his lips. She wants to move but suppresses the desire. *Leonard is quivering and melting.*

When they get to Millersport and dock the boat, Chip takes ice cream orders. He and Annie will carry the cones back. Breck says, "Butter pecan."

Paula calls, "Chocolate is my favorite, but I don't want to wear it so make mine vanilla."

Annie chooses orange pineapple and Chip's favorite is black cherry. They eat their cones on the dock. They don't want to risk any tell - tale accidents making the boat sticky.

While they are enjoying their ice cream, Breck says to Chip, "I got a surprise for you. You know how Dad is about one day at a time and everything depends on his mood?"

"Yeah! So?"

"I had duplicate keys made for the boathouse and the boat. One night when we think it's safe, we'll sneak the boat out. I have to pass Dad's test a couple of times first. Neat, huh?"

Chip says, "I can't believe you did that. Getting caught is definitely a cause for concern."

Paula listens and mentally turns that information over. *Ooh – I don't want any part of that one. Breck seems afraid of his dad on the one hand but rebellious on the other. I don't want him to get into any trouble. I'm scared for him. Furthermore, I won't be getting in his dad's boat again. I don't even want close to his dad's wrath. I get more of the feeling of 'daring-do' and the 'just push me – pull you' fear feelings that the boys have. Breck seems to be taking a step toward freedom by just getting the keys made.*

Captain Breck says, "OK! Everybody back in the boat. Next stop, towpath."

"Aye-aye, sir," the girls comply.

"Virgil Dempsy is quite the sleuth. If there is any tell-tale evidence, Dad will find it," Breck says. "He delights in making my life miserable when he can. Any excuse will do and he's a past master at punishment."

At just about 10:47, Breck slows the engine and pulls toward a dock on the west side of the Yacht Club. Chip hops out. "Come on. Give me your hand, Annie. ... Paula ... See you gals after work."

"Thanks, guys. It was fun. Definitely makes up for Blue Goose. See ya tonight," the girls agree.

Annie and Paula stop at the Lake Breeze Hotel to use the bathroom. Paula pushes her hair back behind her ears. She is missing her locket.

"Oh no! What am I going to do? I don't want Mr. Dempsy to find it and get Breck in trouble. Help me out here, Annie."

"How about this? When the guys go by the snowball stand, see if you can get the $2^{nd}$ boathouse key from Breck. Hurry down there by yourself and see if you can find it in the boat. I'll send Jessie to cover for you. If Dad comes before you get back, I'll tell him you felt sick and went to the

85

bathroom. If you still aren't back, I'll tell him you had to go home for sanitary napkins. I'll cover."

Mr. Harper comes back early to open. Annie is caught off guard and says, "Daddy, we need sanitary napkins and have to go home. Jessie is already at the snowball stand."

"OK, honey. No rush. See you when you get back."

**LAKE BREEZE RESORT**
Buckeye Lake, Ohio

"Whew! So far, so good. Since I don't have to cover for you, I'll go with you. Let's go find the guys." Annie says.

With both girls freed up to be together, they could make plan adjustments if necessary. They head to Breck's house thinking Breck and Chip might be there already. They don't get very far. The guys are in the parking lot of the Lake Breeze Hotel. It took a while to talk Breck out of the key to the boathouse. When he realizes the possible danger in his dad's finding the necklace, he decides it is best to trust Paula to do the job herself. Breck gives her specific instructions when he realizes she has never been in the boathouse. Breck feels he has to be home in case his dad arrives so he can stall Mr. Dempsy.

   "OK," Breck takes a deep breath and tells her, "Go to #8. The boat is hoisted above the water so that it doesn't bang the clapboard floor when the boats make wakes on the lake. Go to the far side of the boat. You will find there are three loose grommets in the tarp covering the boat. Undo two more and you will be able to crawl in. There's a little step stool covered with carpeting near the boat. Use it so that you don't slip and hurt yourself."

   "Gawd! Breck! Do I need all these details?"
   "Yes, you do. You don't know my dad. He will notice anything that isn't exactly right. So, to continue, under the boat cushion in the back seat is a small flashlight. If your necklace is there, once your eyes adjust to the darkness, the flashlight should give you enough light to find it. Good luck. Please, don't call attention to yourself. Please, try not to let anyone see you go in. Lock the door once you get into the boathouse. That way the door won't squeak open and cause anyone to notice. You can give me back the key sometime later today when I see you. Don't make a special trip to find me. Just keep it casual. I'm giving you the copy so I can give Dad his original whenever I see him."
   "Aye, aye, sir," Paula says as she salutes.

Breck looks exasperated. "I hate being so fussy. I don't get to take the boat out very often. When I do, everything has to be just so and with only the person Dad says I can take out. That's why I didn't have you girls meet us at the boathouse."

"OK. Sorry. I just didn't understand. I will be meticulous about every move." She squeezes his arm. "Thanks, Breck."

Breck, Chip and Annie continue through the Lake Breeze Hotel parking lot. Paula doubles back to the boathouse. She doesn't see anyone she knows. Everyone looks like the carefree fun loving vacationer. She pretends she is looking at stones and billboards in order to look nonchalant. … #8 is finally in sight. Paula has the key in her sweaty palm. She glances around, and seeing no one, she lets herself in. Once the door is closed and locked behind her, darkness blinds her.

The sound of water slaps against the pilings. The heat and humidity make it hard for Paula to breathe. The musty smell, the hemp odor, plastic and the smell of polish make her queasy. The dank air feels thick enough to slice. Paula edges her way by Braille to the nose of the boat. She works her way down the other side toward the back. She muffles a groan and lets loose a few swear words when she stubs her toe and trips over a metal object. Strains of "Harbor Lights" are coming from the Pier Ballroom. She needs to focus. She nearly falls over a pile of boat cushions and canvas in the front corner of the boat slip.

Paula's heart is racing. Needing to hurry but also aware of needing to be careful, she can't afford to make any mistakes. Paula finally feels the spot where Breck said the grommets are missing. Working two more lose the way he told her to do she decides she has cleared enough room to let herself into the boat. Paula puts the stool in place to avoid slipping. Going in head first, she slides across the seat cushions. Pulling the tarp cover back over her head Paula is relieved that the tarp sags a bit letting a little air in when a boater speeds past and creates a bit of wind. She reaches for the flashlight. She lets out a sigh of relief that everything is EXACTLY where it is supposed to be. Clockwork! Paula relaxes.

Turning on the flashlight she scans the cushion while feeling the seams. No luck. She whispers a quick prayer to St. Anthony, patron saint of lost articles. She shines the light to the floor, which is covered with raised slats to keep feet out of any water on the boat floor. Wait! A sparkle of gold. Not only is her necklace here, but a single earring as well. While trying to retrieve them, she snags her chain on a slat splinter. Paula works carefully so she doesn't break the chain. She manages to get both pieces of jewelry and slips them into her blouse pocket. There is a noise at the door. Uh oh! "Nature boy, a very strange enchanted boy," Nat King Cole sings. She strains to hear a key work the door lock. She douses the flashlight and shoves her shaking body into a fetal position on the slats of the boat floor. She listens. *Leonard, frozen in place, feels like a knot in Paula's stomach.*

"Shhh! A male voice says. "There's some pillows in the corner we can lay down on. Then I can hold you."

*Who is that?* Paula wonders.

As cushions and canvas are dragged, Paula gets a whiff of something pungent drifting through the loose grommet openings of the tarp as a welcome breeze travels through the boathouse. The man gives instructions to someone. Paula recognizes the voice of Mr. Dempsy. She exhales in a rush and suppresses her urge to cry. She hears wrestling of canvas and cushions. *Who does he have with him?* Paula makes an effort to control her breathing. Slow, easy, and quiet like her swim in Little Lake. *Why is Mr. Dempsy there in the dark?* Then she hears a small female voice say, "Ouch! That hurts. They are sore."

He says, "Shhh, I know, honey. Next year you will be fully blossomed into a young woman. Then your little titties won't hurt anymore."

Paula puts her fist in her mouth and bites to keep silent. What she is hearing shocks and scares her. There is more scuffling of canvas. Paula is still unclear about what is happening. She is worried that they plan to take out the boat. She relaxes when that doesn't seem to be their agenda now that Mr. Dempsy and the girl are doing something that takes their concentration. Paula continues to try to figure out just what is happening.

Then, Paula hears him say loudly and gruffly, "Here! Take it like you did last week."

*What does he want her to take?*

The girl says, "Daddy won't like this. He says he's the only one I can do this with, because he loves me. ... I don't even like it anyway."

Paula has odd sensations in her own breasts and in her lower stomach that she's never felt before. She hears the girl make choking sounds. *Is he hurting her?*

At the same time she is feeling like a rush of wings flutter through her own body and her shorts are suddenly wet.

Paula hears Mr. Dempsy say in a gruff whisper, "Remember! I promised you a snowball and a corn-dog." He had trouble getting the words out because he was breathing so heavily. Under the tarp in the boat, all becomes black and silent. *Leonard leaves.* Paula faints.

Paula eventually returned to a state of awareness. She lies in a cramped position, but at least she is no longer fearful. The tension is gone as are the intruders. She lies there for a while testing her senses. She listens carefully.

It seems safe to move at last. … Paula risks uncovering her head and shoves back the canvas for more fresh air. Her eyes are quite accustomed to the dark by now. She hears a mouse squeak and scamper on the floor boards. When there is no audible response, she slides out from under the boat cover and climbs over the edge, dropping quietly to the floor. She checks her pocket. Yes! She still has the necklace and earring. She manages to undo the clasp, slip the chain around her neck and secure the fastener. Although she wants desperately to be out of there, she knows she must slow down and cover her tracks so that Breck won't get into trouble with his dad.

She takes a few minutes for reflection.

*Who was that girl Mr. Dempsy had here with him? She said that she didn't like what he was doing. It seemed like he had done before whatever he was doing to her. There was the promise of a reward. She stayed without a struggle and does as she's told. Yet, what could she do? She could have been afraid of him . . . afraid to defy an elder. I don't know. Doesn't seem right to me.*

Paula feels quite certain they won't be back today. There was the mention of snowball and corn-dog. She is glad she is not working.

Paula takes her time to be sure everything is as it was when she entered the boathouse. She unlocks the door and listens. No talking or sound of traffic is coming to or from the towpath. Just the strains of "Nola" coming from the Pier ballroom. Paula chances letting herself quickly and quietly from #8 so expertly that one would think she had done it a thousand times. There was no one of consequence in sight except a child playing in a small pile of gravel separating out the pretty stones.

Paula locks the door and walks over to the child. "Hi!" she says. "Are you finding some lovely ones?"

The little girl looks up and shakes her head, "I love the blue ones. There aren't very many of them, but there are some sparkly ones that are nice."

"Yes," Paula agrees, "My favorites are the pink ones that I used to find in the alley behind my house. That alley gave up some real treasures. I, too, like the sparkly ones. Do you live around here?"

"No, my family is visiting my aunt. We live in Lancaster."

"Well, my little rock buddy, my name is Paula and I work in the snowball stand in the park. You come by and I'll treat you to a snowball. Deal?"

"Yeah. I like the blue ones."

"What's your name?

"Heidi. Can I call you Paula?"

"You may. I've got to run. Bring your collection to show me, OK? I'll fix you a blueberry snowball."

"I will. Bye!"

Paula exits the area by way of the steep steps descending from the hotel. She is a counter. Twenty-five steps puts her into the parking lot. She finally takes a look at her tired but working watch. It's been two hours. She needs to hurry home and help with supper. Ahead of her she sees the rest of her friends.

"Hey. Wait up!" she calls.

They stop and turn when they hear Paula's voice and they wait. Annie says, "I saw Dad. He said we don't have to cook tonight unless we want to. He's taking Rusty out to eat. They're invited by someone Dad met at the park."

Breck asks, "What took you so long? Did you have any trouble?"

"No. Everything was exactly where you said it would be. I stubbed my toe on an anchor or pile of hemp. I'm not sure what it was, but I had to howl into my fist. I haven't checked it yet, but it really hurt."

"More importantly," asks Chip," Did you find your locket?"

"I did." Paula shook her head.

"Well, what took you so long?" prods Annie.

"I think I fainted from the heat. Besides, it takes patience to look casual and nonchalant. I met a little girl, Heidi. She is now my rock collecting buddy. She thinks 'Paula' is a nice name so she asked permission to call me 'Paula.'"

"So, Paula it is, huh?" asks Chip as he reaches out to pull her closer to him. The others dodge breaks in the parking lot surface and kick stones. Annie knows how easy it is to turn an ankle.

"Yep! The important thing is that I got the mission accomplished without so much as a raised eyebrow from anyone. Everything is A-OK."

Relieved, Breck says, "My dad got home early. He and mother are going to take the boat out. I'm sure it's because he wants to check how I left it. No dings. No scrapes. Full tank of gas and all."

Paula thinks, *Maybe it wasn't his dad in the boathouse.*

"When are they going for a boat ride?" she asks.

"Later this evening. Dad said he had an errand to run first." Breck was much more relaxed now when he talked about his parents taking the boat out.

Paula blushed but no one noticed her red face. She said nothing about the intruders. She thought for sure the guy was Mr. Dempsy, but she didn't want it to be him. She has no idea who the young girl is. All she wants to do is to go home and take a warm bath and collect her thoughts. Maybe, she should do something with what she knows. ... Maybe not. Would the young girl be helped if Paula told someone? She'd think about it in the tub.

The foursome made their way across the parking lot. The tarmac was hot and bubbly in places. They stopped at their hangout – the Bus Station – for a Coke. J1 and Jed Honesty are in the biggest booth. They rearranged themselves quickly so that Chip and Paula could sit together. There seems to be an unstated understanding that Paula is Chip's girl. She never discusses her relationship with anyone nor between themselves for that matter. They really wouldn't know what to say or how to say it anyway.

Chip asks Jed, "Not delivering ice tonight?"

Chip's mother took their orders. "Cokes, a huge bag of chips. Coming right up."

Jed says, "No. Nobody needs any yet. A bit closer to the 4th and everyone will want ice, so I'm taking a break now."

Paula is pensive. Jed asks, "Hey! Where you at?"

Paula didn't answer but made more of an effort to be with the gang instead of out in left field someplace.

J1 says, "Breck. Your folks are here."

Breck turns and waves to them. They come over to the booth to say, "Hi" and give each of them a candy bar.

"You on your way to the boathouse?" asks Breck.

"Yes," his dad affirms. "You boys have any trouble with the boat this morning?"

"No. She purred right along. I bought a full tank at Hunts Landing.

Paula feels the blood run from her head. She feels faint again. When she hears Mr. Dempsy's voice, her suspicion is confirmed but ... *who was the girl*? She wonders. She's not sure she really wants to know but the whole event is stuck in her gut. *Leonard turns over a couple of times.*

Mr. and Mrs.Dempsy are now at the checkout counter. He says to the cashier, "A pack of Herbert Tarrytons and a pack of Kools, three Pepsi's and a Mounds bar. Is that what you want, Collie?"

"Uh-huh" – He was busy looking at the comic books.

Breck says to anyone who will listen, "Sure is cooler in a motor boat than in this heat. The air isn't going anyplace. What happened to the fan?"

The soda jerk hollered, "Broke. Come back tomorrow."

The Dempseys wave goodbye and leave.

Jed says, "You sit here long enough and the whole damn town shows up. Here comes Debby Jackson. Wonder what she's been up to."

J1 says, "No good, is my best guess."

She passes by their booth. She is finishing off a blueberry snowball. Paula hardly has time to notice anything when she gets a whiff of the same pungent odor she smelled in the boathouse. Paula quickly exits the booth and runs out of the Bus Station to vomit. Chip follows her to see what's the matter.

After Paula finishes retching, Chip walks her home. Annie and Breck follow about ten minutes later. The guys leave saying they would see the girls after work. Annie nods in the affirmative. She then fixes Paula a glass of baking soda and water. Paula is reminded of her father drinking Sal Hepatica. Anyway, it settles her queasy stomach.

"You aren't pregnant, are you?" Annie asks.

"And when might that have happened?" Paula returns the volley in not too good a tone.

"Just kidding! Just kidding. Bad joke."

Paula confides in Annie. "I passed out in the boathouse. I was hot and scared. I not only found my necklace in the boat, but an earring. It could be Mrs. Dempsy's, but she doesn't wear earrings for a boat ride. It was in the rear versus where I'd expect Mrs. Dempsy to be sitting. Plus, you saw how quick they showed up at the Bus Station. I could have been found if I had been much longer."

"Oh, my gawd! I'm so sorry. I didn't put the heat, the stress and the emotions together. I'm really sorry. No wonder you felt sick. Are you going to feel OK to work tonight?"

"I think I'll be all right. I'd really like a bubble bath though."

Annie fixed bologna sandwiches, potato salad and lemonade. Paula picks at her food. She just wants to hit the tub and be alone with her thoughts. When she enters the bathroom, the tears begin to flow involuntarily and her body shakes convulsively. Remembering the sounds and sensations, the heat and the air, she asks herself, *What should I do with the information from this afternoon? I have no parent to tell. It doesn't fit in with three Our Fathers and three Hail Mary's. I don't want to tell Mr. Harper for fear it will cause trouble in the community and perhaps limit Annie's freedom and mine. I don't want to cause Breck any grief. Maybe I'll go see Fr. Maple. He'll know what to do.*

Paula settles into her bath, which calms her. She puts on clean gray shorts and a fresh yellow blouse. Her third blouse of the day.

* * *

On the way to the park the girls are chatting. Paula tells Annie, "I think I might as well bite the bullet and pay Fr.

Maple a visit. Mother keeps asking if I have let him know I am here for the summer."

"Well, that's a shift. What makes you think of him this afternoon? Anything else going on you want to share, Paula?"

"Just the stress of the day is all," Paula assures Annie. "Mother keeps asking and I keep saying that there's been no time. I just want to get it off my list. Mother creates stress with her nagging."

Annie says, "You can always talk to Dad, you know. He's pretty good at listening and problem solving. By the way, I think it's next week that we have another interview with Mrs. Clark about custody. I really don't want anything to upset the apple cart this summer. I'm having too good a time. I don't need any stress either, you know."

"You don't have to worry about anything I say, Annie. We are of the same mind. OK?" Paula assures her good friend as they proceed through the quiet end of the park. Paula gives Annie a hug. They pass the legless guy who sells pencils and suckers. They put some change in his hat and proceed to the stands. Neither of them need any more pencils, but surely he needs the money.

* * *

It is cool and windy that night. Luckily, Paula kept a jacket at the French fry stand. It's colder where she works because the stand is right over the water with no windbreak. There isn't much business. Ted Weims' "Heartaches" played about every tenth song. Even though she loves the song, she doesn't want to hear it tonight. She's trying to get the afternoon events out of her mind

About 9:00 Fr. Maple comes strolling down the path. Since Paula has no customers, she calls him over to the stand.

"What can I do for you, dear?"

"You may not remember me, Father. My name is Paula Bradley. My family is from Perry County ... St. Patrick's church . . ."

"Oh, good heavens, yes. What are you doing working here, Paula?"

Paula tells him what has been going on with her grandparents and parents and why she is staying with the Harper family.

He says, "That's too bad about your grans but good that they have your folks with them. Interesting that you can live here and work. It's amazing how things work out, isn't it? If you ever need to talk about things – you know – if you hit a rocky spot and need to talk, just call me."

"I hoped you'd say that, Father. Actually there is something I want to talk about. Do you have some time tomorrow morning?"

"Sure. I suppose you have to open here. Is 10:00 soon enough?"

"Yes, Father. Thanks. That would be good. Uh, Father."

"Yes."

Paula pauses. "I know it isn't the confessional or anything, but will our conversation be confidential?"

"It can be anything you want it to be. Confidential it is, then. Are you in any trouble or danger?"

"No. I don't think so."

He is somewhat concerned that she said she doesn't 'think so.' "I'll see you at 10:00 with a pot of hot chocolate then. How's that?"

"Just wonderful. Thanks loads. Bye, Father."

He waves as he walks on down the spillway toward Our Lady of Mount Carmel. He has such a nice way about him. No wonder her grans love him so. They hated to lose him to the Lake even though Perry County is just on the other side of the lake. So close yet so far.

\* \* \*

After work, Breck, Chip, Annie and Paula take their usual walk "home." Paula thinks, *I don't know what I'd do without them. Chip is so sweet. Annie is more than a sister to me. I just love her.* In an appreciative mood, Chip is holding her hand and notices she is not her usual gregarious self.

"What's the matter? You having the monthlies?" Chip asks in a private tone.

"No. I'm OK now. I think I was just scared of being caught in the boathouse. It didn't hit me until dinnertime. Then I wasn't so busy tonight so I had time to just remember and replay the day. That's all."

He puts his arm around her and gives her a hug. "I worry about you when you get quiet. Then I know something is bothering you and your folks aren't here or anything."

"Well, I did see Fr. Maple this afternoon. He's an old friend of my family. My mother has been bugging me to see him. Father invited me for hot chocolate and a chat tomorrow morning. I'll go over there and catch him up on what's happening in Perry County. Then I'll go directly to the park to open."

"OK, then. I won't see you until you two get off tomorrow night. I hear he's a pretty neat guy." He gives her another little hug and a kiss in the hair like you'd give a little kid. "Are you warm enough?"

"Yeah! Where did that little kiss come from?"

Chip tips his head to the side then says "I don't know. It just felt natural. Like you needed an 'everything's going to be OK' kiss."

"Maybe everything will be MORE OK with the other kind of kiss."

When she turns around to face him, he kisses her, and she feels his hot body warm up the cool evening. Paula feels her knees go weak and she melts in his arms. *How much emotional experience can a person have in one day!* she wonders.

"That make it better?" he asks.

"Uh-huh. Just one more?" Afterwards she thought, *his first kiss was the sweetest I've ever had but that last kiss made me feel like I did in the boathouse.*

A bit ahead of Chip and Paula, Breck and Annie run into J2. They are almost home when Paula hears him say, "You hear about the parrot that had a string tied around each leg and was for sale in the pet shop?"

Annie says, "No. What is the string for?"

Breck cautions, "Don't encourage him. He knows more jokes than anybody and he'll tell them all night.

"We all know and love the guy. I don't care if he runs through his whole list," Annie says.

J2 says, "A lady comes in to buy him. She asked the owner what the strings are for. He says if you pull the string on his right leg he sings the 'Star Spangled Banner.' If you pull the string on the other leg, he recites 'The Lord's Prayer.' The lady asks, 'What happens if you pull both strings at the same time?' The parrot says, 'I'd fall on me arse, you fool! Awk! Whistle!'"

The gang laughs. The way he tells it makes it funnier than it really is. Especially the 'AWK! Whistle!'

Breck says, "That's all the time you get. No encores tonight. The girls are cold. It's been a big day and we are taking them home. See you tomorrow maybe."

Although Breck seems a little frazzled, he didn't say that there was any trouble at home concerning the day's activity. Chip continues to hold on to Paula like their relationship has jumped up a notch. Paula put her arm around him too, which she had never done until now. It just felt right. *Leonard sighs.* Yes, Leonard is back!

They reach 2nd St. and turn left … Home again . . .
Jiggedy jig! Another sizzling kiss! *Leonard is over the moon.*

Chip says in a whisper in Paula's ear. "Sleep well. Have
a good hot chocolate. I'll see you tomorrow night, OK?"

She nods her head in agreement and gives him a bit of a
wave. The two girls go in to a chilly house, race upstairs for
pj's and a comforter for their bed.

"I think you have something more to tell me," Annie
says

"I don't really know how to explain it very well, but I'll
try." Paula gropes for words to talk about something she
knows nothing about. "I don't know how I'm going to tell Fr.
Maple about my experience in the boathouse and that my
suspicions are confirmed that the man was Mr. Dempsy and
the girl is Debby Jackson. That's really why I want to talk to
him soon. I don't know if I should do something about it or
not. I hope he can tell me what to do. I think if I need to do
something I need to do it right away. You know what I
mean? I can't very well wait through the weekend, can I? I'll
be waiting on customers and hear a song or smell something
that takes me right back to this afternoon and I don't mean
the boat ride. I can't stand it. Even if I think Fr. Maple can
help I've never had that kind of conversation with any adult
let alone a priest. It's just too confusing. I have to be careful
who I tell what. I can't imagine what my mother would do or
Mrs. Clark for that matter. I don't want anything to make any
changes for us."

Annie is shocked and crying. She holds her friend tight.
"I'm so sorry."

# CHAPTER IX
## THE GYPSIES

Davie comes by the house at 9:00 the next morning. Paula is dressing to meet with Father Maple. Davie bangs on the screen door and Annie asks, "What are you doing here, Davie?"

"I got a message for Paula. Where is she?"

"Here I am. What's the trouble?" Paula calls from the kitchen.

"Father Maple says he has an emergency call and can't see you this morning. He'll come by and set up another appointment. He says he's awful sorry. I was afraid I wouldn't get here in time to tell you."

"You did fine, Davie. Come by the stand for your treat."

"No, thanks. Father gave me a treat. I just had to get the message to you on time. So, see ya'!"

Paula shrugs in disbelief that he'd pass up another treat. She waves good-bye as he skips down the road. "I don't know what I'll do now, Annie. What would you do?"

"I don't know. ... See the Gypsies."

Paula ponders the suggestion. She shares stories about the Gypsies with Annie. I tend not to believe everything. On the other hand, I want to believe everything. My mother is from the small Ohio town of Marysville. She told me about the Gypsy caravan coming through town when she was a girl. She said the Gypsies weren't allowed to stop. Supposedly, they take anything that strikes their fancy. If they can wear it or turn it into money, that is good enough. If it exists and they want it, they feel entitled to it.

I have mixed feelings. ... Mother told me about their special colorful wagons they call 'vardos.' One would be a traveling kitchen. They usually camp on the outskirts of town. Mother knew the Sheriff. He told her that when the Gypsies come into the county they are met by the Sheriff and escorted to the next county line. If the Gypsies need to stop for the night, sometimes they're given permission to use the fairgrounds for camping. The Sheriff is there to make sure they stay together. He said they build campfires at night, play music, sing and dance till dawn."

"As far as the Buckeye Lake Gypsies go, I don't know. I keep these collected bits of information to myself. I always check what I hear with what I see. So far, the only thing that rings true is the colorful clothes and the painting on the outside of their tea hut."

Annie says, "These are the only Gypsies I've known. Your mother's account is interesting. Maybe things change for them as they do for us. Life isn't the same for us as it was for our grandparents. At the park, Leah Rose and her sister Donitza keep to themselves. They live in a small house near Hebron with Reon and Davie. I don't know that they ever have any trouble with the law. Donitza looks like she is expecting a baby, but one of them seems to be expecting every season."

Paula asks as she slathers peanut butter on her second piece of toast, "What do they do in the tea hut?"

Annie continues, "As far as I've heard, they read palms, tea leaves and tell fortunes. I can't swear to that because I've never really been interested. ... They've got another place across from the Pier Ballroom. Reon is their brother. He has the High Striker and the 'weight guessing' concession by the entrance of Playland Pier where Breck works. Who knows what Davie will do when he grows up?" Annie grabs two apples and her purse. "Are you about ready to head up to the park?"

Without another word Paula joins Annie and they leave for the park. The girls don't see anyone they know so far. They pass the Pinkie while heading to the French fry stand. Paula adds, "When I pass their tea hut I can see midnight blue drapes and a woven tapestry cloth covering a round table. The cover has what looks like a sun, moon and stars in gold and the whole thing has long fringe on it like a scarf we use to keep on the piano. It takes about five peeks in passing to put the whole picture together."

The girls pass Shiffless and Paula waves, "Hi."

Annie shoves her on the upper arm. "Didn't I tell you not to speak to him?"

"I'm not going to catch anything by waving."

"I don't care. I don't like it. He may think we want to be friendly and we don't."

"All right! I get it. Anyway, right now I need somebody to say my thoughts out loud to. I'm tired of thinking about Junction City, the boathouse and what I heard. These thoughts are chasing each other around in my brain and I'm afraid to talk to anybody. Even though the carnie parents keep an eye on us kids, I don't feel like I can confide in anyone. I'm really just an outsider. Gypsies seem to me like outsiders too. Maybe they'll know what I should do."

Annie nods her head toward Reon. "Reon is friendly to me but seems to draw an imaginary line between what he will talk about and what he won't. He never divulges anything about his way of life or anything else personal. I see him feel ladies' legs before guessing their weight but I never see him with a girl. You won't know any more about him at the end of summer than you know right now. That's my prediction."

"I'm running out of time, Annie. I want an introduction to his sisters. I want my palm read. I want my fortune told. Maybe I can go THROUGH Reon."

They arrive at the stands ready for work. Nothing eventful seems to be happening there. Foot traffic is minimal. After a couple of hours Paula gets a break and tracks Reon down in the park. "Reon, will you introduce me to your sisters? I want my fortune told."

"It depends. How old are you?" He gives her a doubtful look.

"Nuts! Everybody wants to know how old I am." She tells him, "I'm fourteen, going on fifteen."

He shakes his head. "You are too young. I don't think they'll read for you. They might get in trouble with Mr. Turner. It's your age, you know!"

She begs, "Please, Reon. I might be in trouble and I need advice. Please ask them to see me. I'll pay. I have money. I can sneak in. I'll be very careful not to be seen."

"Fourteen!" He shakes his head again. "You wait here. I'll ask."

"Thanks, my friend."

\* \* \*

While he disappears into his sisters' room, Paula stays by the High Stricker going over what she wants. *I need them to tell me I'll have a long and happy life, a good husband and wonderful kids. I want to tell them what I heard that I wasn't supposed to hear because I was where I wasn't supposed to be. I want to tell them who I think did something frightfully wrong and get advice on what I should do. How can I stop carrying this information with me every waking moment? Should I do something public with it or not? Good people don't do those things .... Or do they?*

Paula works herself into a panic. *Leonard is jumping up and down shaking his head, "Yes."*

Reon reports, "They said, 'Yes' and 'They'll send word by Davie.'"

"When?"

"They will get word to you through Davie."

"Thank you. Thank you, Reon."

Paula tries to look casual. She goes into the nearby drug store and looks around. She keeps an eye out for Reon, who makes eye contact and hisses, "I told you they'd send word through Davie."

Paula urges, "I really need to see them soon."

"OK, Here's what we'll do. When no one is looking, go around in back of their building. There are four steps and a little porch. I'll tell Donitza to let you in. I'll get a friend to come in the front door as a paying customer. Leah Rose will pull the black midnight drapes for privacy. Donitza will let my friend out the back when the coast is clear. Can you do that?"

"YES! ... How much does she charge?"

"For a park employee and under aged? She probably won't take anything. She might ask you to give Davie a snowball one of these hot days."

"Agreed." Paula feels like everyone is looking at her. She meanders through the drug store trying not to look suspicious or guilty. When all is clear, Paula heads toward the back of the tea room. She pauses. A hand comes out of a half door.

A voice says, "Come quietly and quickly when you are sure that no one is looking."

Paula makes a slithering move through the darkness behind the door. It takes a minute to adjust her eyes. She shudders. It reminds her of the boathouse.

The woman says, "My name is Leah Rose. Come! Sit with me, Paula."

Leah Rose is incredibly beautiful, five foot five inches tall, with waist length black hair, golden hoop earrings and very large black eyes. She has many bangles on each arm and a large multi-colored crystal ring on her left index finger. Her soothing voice is like a soft wind. The only light is from two burning candles. Leah Rose wears a long maroon broomstick skirt with a gold chain belt that has many coins dangling from it. A blue and gold peasant blouse is gathered across her breast and the gathering ties are loose, dropping the neckline casually low. The room smells intoxicating … better than incense at Christmas high mass. Paula notices a bump in Leah's skirt front. *Yes, I'm sure she is in a family way.*

"Thank you so much for seeing me," Paula says. "I have some money to pay you."

Leah Rose agrees to take a dollar to keep Paula from feeling guilty for taking time from a potential customer. She reminds Paula, "Fr. Maple would not think kindly of either of us if he knew you were here. I told Reon I'd take good care of you. He thinks you are a special young lady. Reon watches over you, you know."

Paula confides, "I didn't know, but I'm glad. I really appreciate it. I didn't think anyone beyond my small circle of friends cared about me. I am an outsider, you know."

"Yes, Paula. I know that and many other things." Leah Rose continues after Paula becomes comfortably seated. "Some of the most unlikely people come to me for advice. We explore what position they could take even if they don't agree with it. What I'm saying is that you do not have to follow my advice. You must decide for yourself what you should do. I'll give you some options to consider. … Ready?"

Paula learns far more this summer than she'd bargained for. She feels a little scared but finally whispers, "I think so."

Leah Rose instructs her, "Lay your right hand on the table with your palm up." She sees that Paula's palm is sweating. Her breath is quick and she can almost hear Paula's heart murmur. "Don't panic, Paula. Just relax. I'm going to talk to you and tell you what I see. When I'm finished, you may ask me questions if you have any. Until then, I am the only one who will talk. You must remain quiet."

Leah Rose is still for a while. Then she says, "First of all, you will live to be an old woman. I see two husbands and seven faithful and wonderful children. Because of the size of

108

your family and employment conditions you will go through some hard times. You eventually come out a winner. This is in your future. ... However, your past shows a rocky relationship with your mother. She is not a well person. You have gained much personal strength through the years as a result of her behavior toward you. You are good, kind and loving. I see a beautiful foundation for a happy life. ... As far as your present is concerned, you are basically happy and peaceful, but you miss your family. You've had a difficult time recently. ... I see a funeral, a family reunion of sorts. Your mother misses you very much and tries to convince you not to return to the lake. ... You are young still. You have much to learn about life and what makes people happy. You will learn tolerance, compassion and your own limitations."

Leah Rose draws a quick sharp breath and places her hand over her mouth. After a moment she says, "That's ALL I will tell you."

Paula reminds her, "You told me I could ask questions." Both are perspiring with no air circulating. It is very hot in the darkened room.

Leah Rose responds, "I've already answered unasked questions. Concerning the experience you recently had which is worrying you, consider it a brutal life's lesson. What you heard and saw was accidental. Nothing good will come of your telling anyone. Share it in confession and take Fr. Maple's advice. There are all kinds of people and all kinds of life experiences. I'm sorry you were unprepared for this one. Remember this, everything in life is as it should be. You must treat life's happenings as lessons from the almighty Eternal One."

"When you see me, pretend you do not know me. This is for our protection. I will never acknowledge that I read for you or even that I know you."

She turns and calls, "Donitza, please show Paula out."
Leah Rose gives Paula a hug.

"Thank you so much, Leah Rose. If you have the time,
could you possibly teach me to read tea leaves? I do
appreciate everything you have told me."

Leah Rose cups Paula's face tenderly in her hands and
whispers, "I don't need tea leaves. It is my gift I share with
you. Now hurry on, sweet child … and be careful."

Paula leaves through the back half door without
incident. She feels good on the one hand, but anxious on the
other. She is especially disturbed about Leah Rose's gasp and
closing the reading so abruptly. Paula gets no response from
Leonard. She did get a lot of information and decides to take
one thing at a time and follow Father's advice, whatever it
will be.

# CHAPTER X
# FATHER MAPLE

On the way back to the stand Paula sees Fr. Maple coming up the towpath. He stops to apologize and reschedule their appointment acknowledging her sense of urgency. "I have some errands to tend to. Can you come to the parsonage later this afternoon? We'll have hot chocolate and I can give you my full attention. Did Davie see you in time?"

"Davie did come to the house while I was still there. Thank you, Father. ... I can come at 3:00 if that's okay."

"We will make it okay." Father agreed. He gives her a hug and waves her back in the direction of the park.

Paula knocks on the door of Our Lady of Mount Carmel parsonage at about five minutes after three. Father Maple himself answers the knock. "Come in! Come in! ... Just to ensure confidentiality, I gave my housekeeper the afternoon off to run some personal errands." He keeps talking as he leads the way down the center hall corridor. "How long have you been here at the Lake, Paula?"

"It's been about three weeks, Father. Seems like longer than that. I guess that since the summer is short, friendships are formed quickly and the new life begins its own agenda." she reasons aloud.

"That makes sense. ... I never really thought about it. Have a seat at the kitchen table, honey. Hmm, I hope honey is on the grocery list. I'll pour, you talk. Tea OK? We seem to be out of cocoa."

"Yes. Thank you, Father." He pours and moves a stack of papers he had been working on, then sits across the table from Paula.

When Paula feels comfortable, she begins, ..."Well, I went for a boat ride with my boyfriend and another couple. Only the two boys were supposed to be in the speedboat. ... We are all really good friends. ... The guys picked us up at a

111

designated place. All went well with the exception that during a speedboat maneuver I lost the locket my grandmother gave me. I didn't discover it was missing until the boat had been docked in the boathouse and everything was put away. ... We all knew Breck would be in trouble if his dad found my locket. I understand his dad is quite strict with him. I mean he punishes Breck at the drop of a hat, so to speak."

"I can see that this could produce a stressful situation for you," Father acknowledged. "Did Breck return to look for the locket?"

"No. He was due home by a certain time and we didn't figure it would take me very long. It was either there or it wasn't. After much pleading he gave me the key to the boathouse."

Father interjects, "Sounds like everything is proceeding in a logical manner. Did you find your necklace?"

"I only wish things were as simple and easy as you make it sound, Father. First, Breck had to give me detailed instructions upon entering and locking the door behind me."... Paula started to shake. She takes a sip of tea to calm herself down. ... "I was already in the boat when I heard a key in the door-lock. ... I was so scared."

Tears well up in Paula's eyes. Father senses he is walking on thin egg shells. This obviously isn't the end of the story. She now has his full attention. It seemed like a casual visit at first but now has turned very serious.

"Paula, Can you tell me what you did when you were alerted that someone was about to enter the boathouse?"

Paula nods her head and wipes her eyes with the back of her hand and continues. "I scooted down on the floor and lay quietly, hoping not to be found. A man comes in with a young girl. They must have nestled on a pile of canvas and kapok cushions that I tripped over when I came in. It was very dark in there." Paula stifles a sob. ...

"Whatever he's doing to her, the girl says, 'Daddy won't like me doing this.' ... Her voice sounded like a whiny young girl. ... The man just keeps sweet-talking her. ... She cries softly. The sounds were more like whimpering. ... I think I must have passed out ... I was so hot and scared"

She takes another drink of tea and Father Maple refreshes her cup asking, "Were you caught?"

She shakes her head and continues, "When I became aware of where I was, I just lay quietly to see if anyone is still in the boathouse. ... All is quiet except for a mouse scampering on the dock. It seemed safe at this point to move undetected. ... I've never been so scared, Father." ... Paula takes another sip of tea. ... "Besides finding my necklace, I find an earring. It is very fancy like someone would wear for a special date. I can't picture Mrs. Dempsy wearing that kind of earring. In the time I have lived here I've never known the Dempsys to do anything but take the boat out and they would be wearing casual clothing. I can't think of any reason why Mrs. Dempsy would be in the boat wearing that earring, IF it is hers. I try not to even think about that."

"Why do you say Mrs.Dempsy?"

Paula is more composed now as she tells the rest of the story. "Well, it IS the Dempsy boathouse and boat. Their son, Breck, is my girlfriend's boyfriend. I didn't really want to mention any names but it just slipped out. Anyway, I don't know what to do with all this information. I haven't told anybody. I'm sure I know who the people are. I don't think I have committed any sin here, have I, Father?"

"No, No. ... Go on." He tells Paula. "Are you saying you think the man is Mr. Dempsy?"

Paula says "It WAS Mr. Dempsy. He has the key. He knows his way around in the dark. It's HIS boathouse. Most importantly, when we four stopped for cokes at the Bus Station, the Dempsys came in. When I heard his voice ordering cigarettes I recognized the voice immediately as

113

being one and the same. ... I really didn't want it to be him ... Don't you see, Father. I don't know what to do. I don't know what to think. I'm afraid to be in Mr. Dempsy's company because I don't know how to act."

Paula gets herself worked up again and starts quivering. *Leonard is right there with her. If he could just stay quiet, so could she.*

What do you think, Father? Do I need to tell the police?

"No, Paula. ... But since you know something no one would like you to know, that may be another matter. Let's think this through. Do you think you are responsible to make things right for the girl?"

"I kind of do, Father, but I'm afraid to report it." Paula is restless and her hands start to shake again. She tries to take another sip of her now cold tea. It's hard to keep the cup from clattering against the saucer.

Father Maple begins thinking out loud. "Now, then, we don't have police here like you do back in Columbus. We have a sheriff and the state highway patrol. So let's review their jobs? The patrolman takes care of traffic problems concerning the highway.... The sheriff likes to keep the peace at any cost. If someone were breaking a law, plain and simple, he'd arrest him. I'm trying to think what the law might be that would have been broken here. I don't really know." Father refreshes their cups while continuing. "The behavior is surely a sinful one and worthy of confession if the man were a Catholic.... Yes ... I can see why this is a burden for you."

Paula nods her head while he continues his reasoning aloud. Father gets up to fill the sugar bowl. ... "You see, Paula, you might say that you are out of your element here. The population at the Lake during the summer is very different from the population that lives here the rest of the year. What you were made aware of is a behavior that you might never have been aware of had you remained with your family and experienced their customary surveillance. ... Are you following me?" Father returns the sugar to the cupboard and rejoins Paula at the table.

"Yes, I think so, Father. Are you saying that what they did was all right?"

"No. No. ... Not at all. I'm saying that what you heard and assumed was being done was happening in the dark and in the privacy of the boathouse to create an aura of secrecy. You were someplace you weren't supposed to be. If you weren't there, likely no one would know about the event. This happening was between the two of them. If the girl found herself in a compromising position, it is regretful. Not your fault. ...

Paula responds indignantly, "So, does one just say it's regretful and that's the end of it? Isn't there anything she can do?" Paula asks, feeling a sense of helplessness and hopelessness for the victim. "I can't believe she wants this to happen. I think she is afraid not to do as she is told."

"What can she herself do? She has the option of telling her parents. ... If she does, her parents may blame her. Her father might take matters into his own hands and go after the guy. There is no law that will deal with this behavior to my knowledge. If there is a law it will not likely be enforced. If the man's behavior becomes public knowledge, the guy's wife might divorce him, leaving a broken home, public shame, and much pain in its wake. Her father might even kill the guy. There IS a law against murder."

Paula gasps. Her eyes go large with surprise as she covers her mouth with her hand. She begins to register the seriousness of her discovery and the potential danger that exists for her. She and Leonard are frozen in place ... speechless.

Father Maple, seeing her reaction quickly continues. "Let's explore a bit further and see if we can find some peace of mind for you. You know something no one would like you to know ... not the man ... not the young girl. ... I can understand how shocking this is for you. You don't even realize the potential danger that you could be in if this story is made public."

Paula nods her head while he continues his reasoning aloud. "Had you remained with your family you would still be innocent of this kind of behavior. ... If there is a public scandal involving you, your parents will likely collect you and take you to Junction City to be with them. ... Of course, if you would rather be with your parents, you could request to be with them without any other reason other than being homesick and missing them . . . ."

Paula regains her composure. "No way! My mother lives her life through me anyhow. She gets involved and makes my problems her problems. It rarely has a good ending. I want a way to have peace within myself and not feel guilty about not doing something if I should do something. You know what I mean?"

Now, Paula is crying. She is seeing the far reaching implication of this afternoon's experience could have for her.

Father puts a hand on her shoulder and gives Paula a napkin for her tears ... "I'm afraid nothing will erase your experience, honey. That may turn out to be emotionally more harmful for you if you leave the lake than staying here and praying to ask God for healing and forgiveness for everybody."

Paula nods and asks him how she can cope with all that's happened.

"Yes, indeed, and that is what I'm trying to help you with, sweetheart. I think what we need at this point is some perspective here. The residents are fairly stable. There are doctors, lawyers, merchants and chiefs as it were. The war affected people's values and morals. Long separations affected people's relationships. Husbands and wives strayed from their marriage vows but reunited when the war was over."

Paula says, "I know! A family I babysat for had that problem. The baby's mother was not faithful. They did manage to save their marriage but things were different between them from then on."

Father agrees, "That's exactly right. The end result of unfaithfulness is a lack of trust. Lack of trust affects their loving bond, sometimes destroying it completely. ... a very difficult counseling process."

"Before you continue, Father, could I use the restroom?"

Father shows Paula the necessary room down the hallway. While she's gone he reheats the water and checks the cookie jar. Empty! He had no idea what the afternoon had in store for him.

Paula arrives refreshed and Father Maple says, "For my part, I can only listen and believe me I have heard all sides. I try to advise, teach and encourage prayer. I want you to understand that YOU have no personal responsibility to do anything in your situation. You need to look at this incident as one of life's most cruel lessons,... YOU have done all YOU can do. You will get no feedback from me. You will not know the results of anything I do. I will take your burden. I will handle things here at the lake. I will be watchful of behavior and wield all the power I can to see that the girl is protected. Do you understand me?"

"Yes, Father. That takes the worry off of my shoulders. So, that's what my Dad means when he says, 'it may not be right, but it's so!'"

Father nods his head. His hall clock strikes 4:00.

"I must get to work, Father. I feel much better. I have more of an understanding now of how life works. This whole experience here at the Lake has been an education that I could not have imagined. ... When school starts in

117

September, I doubt I'll include everything in my essay about 'what I did this summer.'" Paula shakes her head in disbelief.

That was a bit of comic relief they both needed to end this counseling session. Paula promises to give his regards to her relatives and tell them how much he misses his former St. Patrick's parish in Junction City.

Father ends their counseling session. "With the holiday coming up, you will be very busy and I am never sure what the crowd will bring ... emergencies, real or imagined. I want you to feel no guilt at all about the situation. You can go on with your summer in peace." He gives Paula a hug and his blessing.

*Leonard is quiet. He also has found peace.*

\* \* \*

As Paula walks toward the snowball stand she's thinking, *I am sure getting my share of hugs lately. It eases my hunger for Chip's hugs but they are different. I couldn't possibly ever get enough of them.* She shivers when thinking of him. *I feel warm and chilled at the same time. I can't even begin to explain how it's possible. I only know his hugs make me feel so good, so comfortable, so safe and so needed. I look forward to more every night.*

# CHAPTER XI
## THE FUNERAL

As Annie and Paula are getting ready for work, Paula sees her Aunt Esther's green and black, square-roofed 1928 Pontiac pull up in front of the cottage. The design abandoned most traces of the stage coach. The Pontiac still turns heads when it's driven down the street.

Howard Macy gets out. Paula catches her breath and backs up a step.

*"Uh oh! Why is he here?" Leonard wonders.*

"Hi, Paula. I'm here to collect you and your things. Your granddad passed away yesterday and your folks want you in Junction City for the funeral."

\* \* \*

The delivery of the information is so matter of fact. Paula sits in a chair to collect her thoughts for a minute.

*Leonard's activity goes into front and center. Does he expect her to just grab some clothes and get into the car and leave town with no parting words telling anyone 'good-bye' or when she might be back. No one knows about her history with Howard. Father Maple emphasized safety for her. Is she being thrown into the lion's den? Leonard pauses for a breath and balance, then says, "Just get in the car as your parents instructed and trust that their decision is best under the circumstances."*

\* \* \*

Annie heard everything from the kitchen. She saves the day as only she can. She comes into the living room saying, "Don't worry about the stand, Paula. I'll tell Dad and we'll be able to get someone to work for you. Probably Jessie." She puts her arms around her friend and begins rubbing her back. This loving gesture means more than words can convey.

Sobbing convulsively, Paula manages to whisper, "I loved my granddad. Life will never be the same without him. Will you stay with me and help me gather what I need to take?"

"Of course." Annie is good at taking charge when she must. She gathers a dress, skirt, blouses, dungarees, socks and saddle shoes holding each item up for Paula who shakes her head 'yes or no.'

"Why does it have to be the Fourth of July weekend? Do you think you all will be OK, down one? You already planned for Jessie to work." Paula, worries about everything both at the lake and in Junction City, then starts to cry again. "I don't know how I'll handle seeing Mother, Dad, and Jeniece after being separated for six weeks. My experience at the boathouse makes me think something like that could happen to me with Howard. I'm leery of being with him since Fr. Maple made such a point of my being safe."

Annie shakes her head in understanding. "Don't worry about anything here. Dad will understand. I'll explain to the guys tonight. Maybe Chip can work for you. As far as the rest of your fears go, I'll be praying for you every minute. Just get it behind you and hurry back."

As the girls approach the car they give each other one last embrace. "See you soon." Paula whispers.

Paula huddles herself in the corner of the passenger seat as far away from Howard as she can get.

"Why are you so quiet?" Howard tries to console Paula. "No one can predict when our last day will be. Even though it is expected, no one is really prepared for it."

Howard has no idea why Paula is so pensive and anxious. He is a family friend of many years. She is remembering a night a couple of years ago, while he lived with her family before he got married. He came home drunk one night and came into her bedroom. He woke her out of a sound sleep with a yucky kiss. He has a really (gag) big tongue. Paula turned away from him and he left her room but the memory remained. She never told a soul. ... She's never trusted him since then. She wonders if he remembers doing that.

"Have you been working every day?" Howard prods.

"Annie and I get Mondays off."

Silence resumes.

"What do you do on your days off?"

"We usually go swimming." *We don't usually, but I don't feel like giving him any information.* "I'd really just like to be quiet and remember my grandpa if it's okay with you?"

"I understand. If there's anything you want to talk about or have any questions, I'll tell you what I know."

Paula nods and closes her eyes. After a short reverie she decides to tell Howard about her relationship with her grandfather.

"Granddad and I used to sit on the front porch swing on a hot summer day armed with fly swatters. We slew 'Philistines.' The flies were something awful in summer."

"Your granddad was quite the character."

"I love him and Maw Emmy. They are also my godparents, you know. I think that makes a special bond for us. I used to get so tickled with Maw Emmy. She has a special relationship with each of her chickens. It is hard for her to choose the one to have the honor of the Sunday stewing pot."

"I suppose that's a regular Saturday task. I never much thought about it," Howard said as he turned onto Route 13 toward Somerset.

"When I was little, Mother never allowed me to stick out my tongue, make an ugly face, or a snoot when I was angry. There was always the threat of corporal punishment looming if I were caught. It was hard to figure out a safe way to be

121

mad around her. She's unpredictable. I remember when I was five, I spent a weekend on the farm. Maw Emmy was fixing Sunday dinner. I was feeling frisky and untied her apron strings."

"She said, 'Paula, don't do that, you little dickens!' I sneaked up behind her and did it again. 'Stop that! Can't you see I'm too busy to keep tying my apron?' A third time brought her full wrath down on me. 'If you do that again, I'll lock you out of the house.'"

"'No, you won't,' I teased. You wouldn't lock me out, would you?' Not heeding her warning, I dared again. She chased me out the back screen door and locked it. She sure did."

"I banged on the screen, ' Let me in, Maw Emmy! I'm sorry. I won't do it again, I promise.' She held fast. There would be no unlocking the screen door for me. I was frustrated not to get my way. I issued the worst threat I could think of. 'If you don't let me in I'm going to make snoots at your chickens. And then I'll tell Grandpa on you.'"

"She sounded like Brer' Rabbit thrown into the briar patch. 'Oh no! *not* snoots at my chickens.' Then she laughed till she cried. When I look back I can see why my threat was so funny. But I was only five."

With my eyes closed I feigned sleep, but I had to smile at that memory.

Howard chuckled as he turned west at New Lexington and passed the "old folks home," a landmark for Paula. They finally reached the catalpa tree-lined lane that stretched from the dilapidated one-room, brick "Rush Creek" school house to the home place.

Paula said, "My dad and all my aunts attended school here."

She admires the little white shingle farm house that sits at least a half a city block's distance from the highway. "I don't know how many times I sat on the porch with Grandpa counting cars in passing funeral processions? 'Why do you count funeral cars, Grandpa?' I asked him. 'Oh honey,' he'd say, 'It gives me a warm feeling to see who will be in the procession when I die.'"

"So now, he'll find out for sure. I'll bet he didn't figure on the folks who are regular customers of Hite's Tavern to come and support Aunt Esther. Or, more to the point, to enjoy the wake. Nobody at Hite's ever passes on a reason for a party. I suppose they'll go back to the tavern and tell everybody who will listen about all they ate, drank, saw and heard."

Howard shook his head yes. "They do that." He grinned.

"There are my aunts' and uncles' cars parked in the field beyond the built-in garage. Other cars are starting to line up in the corn field that hasn't been planted this year. It's hard to tell how far back in the field they'll have to park."

"Well, Paula! Here we are – safe and sound. Are you ready for your folks?"

"Yes. Thanks, Howard, for picking me up at the Lake."

*Leonard is OK with things. So far, so good. The real test comes when she sees her family.*

* * *

Paula makes her way inside the hardened clay floor of the garage which is part of the root cellar. She loves the smell. The garage doors are open to let in the daylight and fresh air. Folding chairs are set up here and there. The lane is strewn with broken bits of clay tile that are painful on bare feet. The little stream runs from Rush Creek School to Rush Creek beyond the house with its yellow stained banks and beautifully clear ice cold iron water. It is always so inviting on a hot summer day. The small feeder stream is nearly dried up. Maybe an inch of water stands stagnant. It is so hot and dry this summer.

Jeniece comes running down the basement steps to greet Paula whom she hasn't seen in a couple of months. "Four of our cousins are already here," she said. "The ones who don't live near are settled in the bedrooms they'll be using."

Paula hugs her sister and greets each cousin lovingly. They are very close. They are more like brothers and sisters to Paula. However, their relationship seems different now. They are young teens and haven't seen each other for close to a year.

* * *

At fourteen, new interests take center stage. Dick and Harry go to St. Charles. St. Mary of the Springs is considered its sister school. Paula is looking forward to talking about 'who knows who.' Marcie Ruth and Bonnie live in Somerset. They are taught by Dominican nuns as Paula is.

"You know, Jeniece, the ten kids in Aunt Mid's family of which Marcie Ruth and Bonnie are the youngest, can't leave the farm 'til they milk the cows. Eggs need gathering and there's always an orphaned lamb or two that need bottle fed. I know the routine."

"There's Maw Emmy." She gives Paula a giant hug and pats her back as Paula sobs in her arms.

"Your mother's in the kitchen and your dad is tapping a keg of Gambrinus in the backyard. If he's finished, he might be ready to give haircuts on the front porch. We have all been anxious to see you."

Jeniece asks, "How does Daddy know how to cut hair?"

Paula feels like the family historian. "He went to barber college back in Chicago during Al Capone days in the 20's."

Paula leaves Maw's embrace and heads up the cellar steps to the kitchen. It smells of boiling chicken and noodles. Her mother removes an apple pie from the oven. Food is

124

beginning to come in from miles around. It's a typical farm wake.

Her mother's stockings are rolled below the knee and she is wearing her black Red Cross oxfords. She wears one of Maw Emmy's aprons.

All the while Jeniece is still by her side. "Who is Al Capone?"

"A gangster and that's a story for another year."

Mother smiles. "Well, there you are! I was just wondering how soon you'd roll in. Have a good trip with Howard?"

Paula reaches her for a brief hug and kiss hello. "Fine," she says.

"Do you have enough clothes for the funeral, Paula?"

"Depends on how many days. I have two changes."

"We'll pick you up something in Somerset. Let's see. No taller! Hair longer! Not as tan as I would have expected."

"The deal is 'to work,' Mother. My Grandview Pool summers are history."

"You've been working every day? Are you getting along okay with the Harper family?"

"Yes, I work every day. Yes, we get along fine. He's a good boss and he watches over us closely. Nice man! Annie and Rusty are fine."

When Dad comes in from the backyard, Paula becomes aware of how much she misses his Popeye arms around her and his smell. He rolls his own Bull Durham cigarettes and keeps the little pouch of tobacco in his left shirt pocket. He smells a tad less than fresh but has a slight hint of Bay Rum on his neck. His sleeves are rolled up above his elbows. His sandy hair and mustache are a sight for sore eyes. She can't restrain a long sigh.

"How's my girl?" They hug long and hard. She sobs and he rubs her back, making everything OK. The parade of cousins starts filing through and Paula wipes her eyes on her dad's sleeve.

Mother says, "Paula, you and Jeniece use Granddad's bedroom next to the kitchen."

A cold chill goes up Paula's back and she whispers to Jeniece, "That's close as we can get to him, I guess."

\* \* \*

After dinner the family goes to the Chute funeral home in New Lexington.

Paula sizes up the situation! Friday with wake following. Back to the Lake Saturday and return to my familiar summer pattern. That's how she thinks it will probably go.

*Leonard has his doubts. Her logic is colored with how she wants it. We'll see!*

There is little time for socializing. The funeral has its own agenda and those priorities are soon to be Paula's. Like it or not.

She pays her respects at the casket, . . . Hail Mary, full of grace, but songs keep going through her mind: *'Ha ha, ha, you and me,'* words to *'Little Brown Jug,,' 'Ole Dan Tucker, you're too late to come to supper,'* and the *'Foggy, Foggy Dew.'* Silent, now, he lay peacefully in his coffin. Lots of flowers. She must remember to count the cars in the funeral procession for him. Paula continues kneeling for a while. She listens to all the old familiar jargon one hears at funerals after leaving the casket.

"Doesn't he look nice?"

"We'll miss seeing him in his church pew on Sundays."

"Maybelle didn't want to come down here, you know?"

"Will Dixie stay at the farm?"

"Did he suffer?"

"Emmy still uses those coffee bag wires to curl her hair."

"Pete and Maybelle's youngest has been going to school in Junction, you know?"

"Dixie, his dog, will pine away." Paula bristles at that one. Dixie is her dog. Granddad was just keeping her for Paula.

"I haven't seen the older one in a couple of years." Paula smiles to herself because they don't recognize her.

Paula tells Maw Emmy, "I didn't think he was Catholic? I always saw him in the back of the church with some guys."

* * *

Paula wove her way through the mourners. She doesn't care. She just wants to sit with Dick, Harry, Marcie Ruth and Bonnie. She knows they'll be here 'til 9:00. She just wants to hear how turning 13, 14, and 15 has changed their lives as it has changed hers.

They sit in a huddle far away from the viewing area. Dick tells the latest moron jokes and Harry imitates his favorite radio personalities: Digger O'Dell, the friendly undertaker, and Clem Cadiddle Hopper. They laughed so loud that Aunt Esther said, "Take your rowdy behavior outside. You aren't being respectful."

They snicker all the way out the door. "...to the briar patch," Paula says.

Aunt Esther says, "Shhh! You'd better shhh or else." She could be stern.

They had to catch up on the latest news about boyfriends, girlfriends, who is driving, which teachers and classmates do they have in common. It is wonderful to see them again.

Paula wants to spend the night with Bonnie and Marcie Ruth, but Aunt Mid says, "It's too complicated. You'll see each other tomorrow."

\* \* \*

The night before the funeral it rained. Paula's Mother says, "The rain is desperately needed, so it's a welcome relief. However, it would have made things easier had it waited till after the funeral. 'Blessed is the corpse the rain falls on.'"

She tells Paula, "Dad Bradley will be buried beside Maudie and Lucy They are sisters on either side of your dad. They died when they were young girls."

"Are those the two girls whose picture is on the wall at the top of the stairs?"

Mother answers, "Yes. We'll talk more later." She reaches out. "Hello, Mrs. Morgan. So nice to see you. How have you been?"

Paula continues conversation with the cousins. "I'm always glad to hear bits and pieces of family history. I think I have the pieces of the puzzle put together and another chunk plops in."

\* \* \*

After Mass at St. Patrick's church next day, the pall bearers must carry the casket about ¾'s of a city block over a wet and slick gravel pathway and saturated ground. The women's high heels are sinking into the wet earth. Father Maple is here from the Lake. Paula is surprised to see him participating. Saying the final prayers at the bier, he invites everyone to lay flowers on the casket. As Paula reaches to place her rose, there's a rush of water and a swooshing sound. The funeral director pulls her away roughly by the arm and announces, "THE SERVICE IS CONCLUDED." He tells Father Maple, "Speed it up, Father."

The mourners learn later that the wall of Maude's grave gives way and her little casket washes into P. Henry Bradley's freshly dug space. Much has to be done to get them properly buried and reburied.

The rain ceases. Friends and neighbors continue to gather at the house. They bring food, tell stories and drink from the tapped keg. There are bottles of pop and beer in iced copper boilers that were used to make moonshine during prohibition. Large blocks of ice are picked into small chunks to cool the drinks. Paula tells Aunt Esther, "I can't imagine what food could be missing from this spread. It's hard for me to stay away from the pickled beets and eggs. "

There's ham, fried chicken, pulled chicken sandwiches, jello-salads, mashed potatoes and gravy, potato salad, home-made bread and butter, cakes and pies. . . . a little slice of heaven.

Paula tells Aunt Mid, "I didn't know how much I miss these foods that have been replaced by French fries and Corn Dogs this summer."

Aunt Mid's family arrives in two identical cars. This year they are baby blue Plymouth sedans. With ten kids and cows that need milking, one car-full of kids always has to leave early. "Cows need milking. End of story. No whining!" Aunt Mid has a variety of sayings. "No days off for farmers." "Where you're wanted a lot, stay little. Where you're wanted little, stay not at all." "Fish and guests stink after three days." Paula never leaves without hearing at least two of them and at least one Pat and Mike story which is Aunt Mid's specialty."

Little by little the crowd thins out. A couple of euchre games are finished. "Maw Emmy, I'll return the cards to the oak secretary in the living room." Paula assures her.

The only families who remain are Aunt Esther (no kids), Aunt Dot's (three boys), and Pete's (Jeniece and Paula). The more beer they drink, the louder they talk. The older ones listen while the little ones go to sleep and are carried to bed.

The conversation goes ". . . I know how hard it was for you, Maybelle. We'll spend time sorting things tomorrow." More anger and bitterness surfaces. Maybelle is the center of it all. Paula thought it was supposed to be a grieving and memorial gathering. It becomes more about her mother's perceived slights and lack of appreciation shown by the aunts who should have been the ones taking care of their dad as far as her mother was concerned.

"No word of thanks to me," her mother says. "My household was disrupted. Why am I the one who had to sacrifice my family? Why was I the one to be left with one daughter just entering high school while the other one was taken from me? Why was I the one who had to join my husband here to cook, clean and do the laundry for HIS parents? I was left high and dry with no choices. I had to come down here to get MY family back. My younger daughter needs her mother. My older daughter is now separated from us. Teenage years aren't easy, you know. 'A man should leave his parents and 'cleave to his wife.' Supposedly she read that in the bible. The beer quotes it many times."

All these angry questions are laced with remarks from the aunts, all saying why it couldn't be them. Paula has heard them all from her mother before. They always go unanswered even before her dad left Columbus. They are chewed like cud. Each time one of the questions comes up, her mother gets no closer to a satisfactory answer. Finally, she just gives in. "Let him go. Let him take Jeniece. I'll stay in Columbus with Paula."

Aunt Dot says, "I couldn't take care of dad. I have a store to run." Aunt Esther asks, "Who will run the tavern without stealing me blind?" It was beginning to sound like the reasons no one would help the little red hen gather and grind the wheat to make her bread.

Daddy finally said, "It was easier for me to come down here and get a job at Clay Tile." This remark again raises Mother's fury. She says, "You just wanted to BE back here. 'You can take the boy out of the farm, but you can't take the farm out of the boy.'" How many times has Paula heard that one?

Aunt Dot cuts in, "God forbid anyone should enjoy what he feels duty bound to do."

Aunt Esther agrees to throw money at the situation. That is usually what she does when she can't personally be there.

After the emotions are spent, the smarting and blaming is over for the time being. Aunt Dot agrees to take Maw Emmy with her to live out her days in Columbus. They have a large apartment over a store. It seems that's all the resolution Maybelle Bradley is going to get.

Paula's mother continues while popping the cap from another 'Black Label.' "I'm washing my hands of the whole damn thing. I've done the best I can do. It's my fault, I guess. When something needs doing, I just do it."

"My golden memories of days on the farm are over." Paula says to Harry, "All I want is to get back to Buckeye Lake as soon as possible because I know that Mother isn't finished with her ranting by any means. She'll continue to thrash it out with Dad 'til he gets sick of it and decks her. That's the usual scenario." She deals out another hand of rummy to the guys.

Little by little the six remaining cousins find their beds and the house quiets down.

## Chapter XII
## The Morning After the Funeral

Next morning the aunts gather what little Maw Emmy wants to take for her comfort: a few clothes, shoes, 'Eight O'clock Coffee' curlers, her prayer book and rosary. Paula's dad, Pete, promises to bring Maw Emmy's rocker to Columbus. One of the neighbors wants to rent the farmhouse for her daughter the following month. Pete agrees to stay on to get the house packed up – the aunts agree to come back down to sort and divide the remains that don't get done the following day. When all have said their goodbyes, Paula is given a surprise.

Her mother is casually cleaning up. She says, "Your playmate, Evie Snyder, from the farm across the road called when she heard you were here for a few days. She asks if you can go on a double date with her and her boyfriend. I thought it would be fun for you, so I said you could go. If you don't want to go you can call her and tell her."

"Where are they going?"

"Evie said they'd either go bowling or roller skating."

Paula is in the process of gathering her things to return to Buckeye Lake. "When do you plan to take me back?"

"We don't have a specific plan yet. There's time to talk about it. We can spend a little family time, get some things organized here and not be too rushed. How does that sound?"

It doesn't sound too good to Paula, but knowing what they'd all been through so far, she doesn't want to rock the boat further. "OK. Are the kids picking me up or what?"

"Evie said they'd be here at 6:30."

Paula thinks, *Typical of mother. She figures it all out ... Puts the plan into action ... Runs it up the flagpole ... See if anyone salutes . . . Oh well! It's Friday. I can finish packing my things tomorrow.*

Evie and the guys show up at 6:35. She introduces her
date, George, and Paula's date, Slim Fetters. They have a
short conversation on choices. The guys really seem to have
decided on bowling.

"I haven't bowled much. I'm not good at bowling. I've
only done it twice," Paula says.

Slim says, "No problem. You'll be 'the best' by the end
of three games."

*Yeah*, Paula thinks. *Just like I was 'the best' after rowing
half way to Blue Goose.*

\* \* \*

Slim is a head taller than Paula and three times wider.
His freckles go with his sandy hair. He is a little on the
clumsy side she judges, when he trips on the porch steps. As
Paula gets into the car she tells herself, *It's just three games
of bowling.* ... She endures the evening. Actually she did
have a good time. As is Paula's habit, she imagines herself
*without Chip but with Slim. Do I want to be here? All the
arguments pro and con I can think of are covered. I can see
myself staying at the farm and dating Slim; changing
schools; getting married; living on a farm of our own;
having a houseful of kids to help run the place.*

She is jolted back to reality when Slim says as they
reach the front porch, "We'll pick you up at 6:30 tomorrow
night."

They already decided to go to the movies. Nobody
bothered to consult Paula. She's none too happy about all
these decisions.

"I'll have to ask my parents. I'm due back at Buckeye
Lake. You may not know that I have a job."

"It's OK. We already cleared it with your dad," Slim
says as they reach the front door.

*Hmmm! It's sounding like a conspiracy.*

*Leonard surmises, The conspiracy hasn't surfaced yet as
she will soon see.*

"I'll call you. 25R4, right?" Slim asks.

"I have no idea. I just know it's a four party line with an
operator and a switchboard out there somewhere. She
connects the two phone lines somehow. Of course the other
three parties hear the ring also. I can just see them all waiting
until the phone is answered so they can pick up for some
hopefully juicy eavesdropping."

Slim laughs as he gives Paula a sideways squeeze for his
parting gesture. "I'll call you."

* * *

Before sleep Paula makes her entry.

Dear Diary, July 8, 1949

The evening was pleasant enough. I bowled 49, 103
and 120. 'The best,' I'm not going to be. That's clear. Slim
gave me pointers by coming too close for comfort behind
me and guiding my grip and stance. I felt like he had
something other than bowling on his mind. By the third
game his hands were sweaty. It could have been exertion,
but in the back of my mind I thought not. It was more
like revving up for something else. I could feel his heart
pounding through his tee shirt.

After we left the bowling lanes, Evie's date says,
"Hamburgers at the Diner?"

The other two jumped in with a resounding, "Yes!"
So, hamburger, fries and Cokes it was. The fries made
me think of where I wanted to be. They had me home by
a quarter to eleven. Slim walked me to the door. At the
Diner they talked about wanting to see, "She Wore a

135

Yellow Ribbon" showing in Somerset. I haven't been to a movie since March.

Alarms are going off in my head from a distance. I'll figure it out.

Later, Paula


Paula hides her diary under her mattress and enters a fitful sleep.

Saturday morning at the breakfast table Paula's dad says, "The movies! A perfect way to spend a Saturday night. Your mother, Jeniece and I might just go into New Lex to visit my cousins. They have kids for Jeneice to play with. We'll be back by the time you get back from the movies."

\* \* \*


That was almost too easy. Paula wonders where Slim and George are getting the money. So far as she knows, they help out at their family farm for pocket money. Not her problem to worry about though. Yet, there goes that alarm again. *Leonard turns over.*

Dear Diary, July 9, Saturday night.

At the movies, I should have thought ahead. Popcorn, hand holding, arm on my seat back. By the second feature the arm eases its way to my shoulder. Rather than focus on the movie, I'm not feeling comfortable. It's not Chip. I'm getting a legitimate headache. All the while Slim is starting to put a little heat in the hand at the end of his arm. It is groping ever so cautiously from my shoulder, easing down my front, retreating at my flinch, then testing again.

I manage to avoid "first base." Again, I did have a good time in spite of fending off his physical advances.

More later, Paula

* * *

Paula is feeling nostalgic about the farm. They'd be closing down the house, but not the memories. Darkness settles in. No street lights. The night sounds are the crickets which she used to think were the sounds the stars made when they twinkled. She laughed at herself. In August there's always shooting stars and the sounds of cicadas trumping the sound of the tree frogs that replace the calliope music at the amusement park.

It's hot and sticky again. The house is still lit by natural gas piped into ceiling fixtures in every room as well as some electricity. If you want to see anything, the seeing had better be done before the sun goes down. Maw Emmy's light is like a propane lantern low on fuel, used while camping. The free gas is a perk for leasing mineral rights to an oil company. The grandparents cook and heat with natural gas. There is a very large grate in the floor between the living room and dining room. That's the only heat source the house has. All the beds are laden with feather ticks and comforters while thick ice forms on the bedroom windows in the dead of winter. Such memories!

There's a special smell about the house this morning from the gas, coffee made with iron rich water, sliced apples drying on newspaper under the tall four legged stove in the kitchen and thick fresh pork side frying.

A rickety windmill sits atop the roof above the dining room that provides just enough electricity to operate the radio. A wire is brought in from under the window sash. Paula learns that it is an antenna. A floor lamp in the living room makes use of that electric power too. Somehow a battery in the cellar is involved. Grandpa operated a hand pump every day to charge the battery. Paula doesn't understand it but that's what she saw.

Up in the dining room Grandpa would lean over the radio with his ear close, so he could get news of WWII through the static. He listened to Walter Winchell calling, "Good evening, Mr. and Mrs. America and all the ships at sea, reporting." Grandpa read a book by Earnest Pyle who told about life in the trenches. The grandparents had at least ten grandchildren serving in the armed forces. One was a paratrooper, one a POW in China, two were Army nurses, Paula's brother was a sailor and the other five were in the infantry. She bows her head in thanks to God that eventually they all returned home safely. It makes her physically ill to this day to think of those kids at age 18 serving on land, air and sea. Many had never been away from home. There is nothing like being homesick. Nothing!

Tomorrow, Sunday, she and her folks will talk. They need to get everything sorted out.

After Mass her mother's plan for Paula finally emerges. She is cooking Maw Emmy's favorite rooster who attacks mother every time she goes out the back door. There's a message there, somewhere, Paula is sure.

"Dinner is so good, Mother. The chicken and noodles are foods I really miss."

Her mother seems detached. "Come help with dinner dishes." She washes, Paula dries. Dad sits at the kitchen table rolling one of his cigarettes. Jeniece is playing with paper dolls in the dining room on the daybed.

Mother takes a deep breath then says, "Your dad and I were talking. We'd really like you to stay with us and not return to the Lake." She put the jam and homemade bread into the pie safe. "You've had a good time with Slim, Evie and her boyfriend, haven't you?"

"I had a good enough time. Those guys can't have that much money to spend. We bowled three games, rented shoes, then hamburgers at the drive in on Friday. Saturday night it was movies and popcorn. They will probably be broke the rest of the month."

Dad put in his 'two cents.' "Well, I helped them out a little. I wanted to be sure you had a good time, honey."

Paula can see the handwriting on the wall. Helping clean, pack and close up the house and babysitting her little sister. No, she's not interested.

"Thanks, Daddy. Nice try. Number one: I already have a boyfriend. Number two: more importantly, I already have a job. I work every day. I made a deal. You guys made a deal with Mr. Harper too – a deal is a deal. There's a month and a half left for the park to be open. I've already missed July fourth, the busiest day of the summer."

Mother is crying at this point. "We haven't seen you at all this summer. We just think it's best for you to be with us now."

"Well, I don't think so."

Mother followed Paula's response with her hand full open and letting her have it on the left cheek. It's like her mother turned on a dime.

"You little slut! I let you out of my sight and you draw boys like trash draws flies. You just want to get back there so you can whore around!"

Paula is stunned. "Where did that come from? I don't know what you are referring to. You must have information I don't have."

Her mother continues name calling and character bashing. Paula is in shock. Nothing could be farther from the truth. *Where does she ever get such an opinion of me?* Paula bolts out the back door toward the hen house, trips and collapses on the little hill beside the hedges across from the chickens, and weeps. *If she thinks that badly about me, why does she want me home?* Paula loses track of time.

*Leonard is in shock too. His small body is hiding in the corner of Paula's being. There are a couple of arrows sticking in the lamb. He's bleeding, twitching and mortally wounded.*

Mother screams at Paula from the back porch. Paula doesn't answer. She just stays there, frozen in place. She can't talk. The ground is turning moist and cool around her. She can hear the rustling of feathered bodies and their gentle noises from the hen house, low pitched, extended bawks. They seem to be talking amongst themselves.

"Move over,"

"Go back to sleep,"

"It's only her." B a w k.

"Quiet down."

"I need my sleep to lay eggs in the morning."

"B a w k." More rustling.

Paula feels her way further into the thicket of gooseberry, forsythia, and other nameless hedgery. She hears footsteps coming up the path. *I know where I am, but I can't see. It's Daddy.*

He's carrying a flashlight and calling her quietly. "Paula, where are you?"

In the flashlight's beam he sees her foot sticking out of the bushes. He lowers himself and wraps his arms around her. He coaxes her to come back to the house. "You were hearing the beer, exhaustion, and anger talking, honey. Your mother doesn't mean all those things she says. She's at the end of her energy. She drinks too much, but it doesn't drown her anger toward Esther and Dot who don't provide enough help for your mother." After a moment or so of silence he says, "Won't you please come back to the house?"

All the while he's stroking her hair like Paula's mentally stroking Leonard. She says, "It sounds like she feels no one understands her or cares."

After some time, Paula agrees to come back to the house. "Can you keep her mouth off of me? Can we leave for the Lake first thing in the morning? I won't stay here, Daddy. I just can't."

"OK. We'll leave about 9:00. I'll have you there by noon at the latest."

Paula goes back with him to a quiet house and hurries upstairs to her bedroom where Jeniece has fallen asleep on top of the white damask bedspread that covers the double iron bed. Paula thinks, *Mother has hurled her last verbal javelin at me. I can't separate her from the beer she drinks to deaden her pain.*

She crawls in under the blankets and moves them to cover Jeniece. *Leonard is still quaking and frightened.*

Paula awakes Monday morning to the sound of the oil well in the distant field and the smell of coffee, bacon and oatmeal. The smell is so comforting. Mother is quiet, remorseful, and keeps busy. Evidently Daddy told her he's taking me back to the lake. No one mentions last night. She's glad not to hear anything her mother has to say – good, bad, or in between.

# CHAPTER XIII
# A DEAL IS A DEAL

On the way back to the Lake Paula and her dad talk. Actually, she talks and he listens. "You know, Daddy, I didn't want to accept the four-year scholarship to St. Mary's. I was talked into taking it. A month before school started you and Jeniece moved to Junction City. It wasn't a happy year in school for me. Mother was sick and I was anchored to the house with her. I missed getting acquainted with my classmates. Then I get permission to live with the Harper family after Mother decides to join you. This permission was for YOUR convenience or you wouldn't have let me go. So, after I make my adjustment and like it, 'Bad girl! Bad girl!' I am having a hard enough time making sense out of life. All I end up with is pain and confusion. I feel so heavy. Is life really supposed to be this way?"

He says, "Honey, we all do the best we can. I thought that for you to accept the scholarship was in your best interest in the long run. Yes, we made a deal and you are right. It is right that we honor the deal. We have things we have to do to wrap up the two Junction City houses. Then we'll take back our house in Columbus and have your room ready for you to come home by Labor Day. I'll pick you up so you won't have to take a bus."

In the silence Paula is thinking ...*who would think a funeral would be so memorable? Somebody said, the truth is stranger than fiction. The smells, the blackberry scratches, chickens, Rush Creek,, catalpa trees and the burning of blessed beeswax candles invoke my senses and take me to a place of love and comfort. My lamb is quiet now. He is resting and healing.*

Sometimes a question comes up about Dad's life in the Rush Creek one-room schoolhouse and the present farm house that replaced the burned-out house where the chickens now reside. I want to know more about his blind Aunt Mandy and his Uncle Hugh. I told him the latest about Fr. Maple. He is happy that Father and I are friendly and that I go to confession and communion regularly. He is confident I am more secure than he assumed I was. It seems to cancel the perceived notions my mother entertains. Regular confession and communion should be a message for both of them.

"Mother lives her life through me, Daddy. It's irritating. Sometimes I make up stories that could be my life. She reads my diary so I try to entertain her. However, there is no information that would lead to her current conclusions."

\* \* \*

When they arrive at the Lake, no one is home. Paula puts her stuff away and her dad walks her to the park. Paula pleads as they pass by, "No Pink Elephant. Please, no drinking, OK?"

"OK, I promise."

Yep. Rusty and Mister Harper are in the French fry stand. *Leonard is very happy.* Annie is in the snowball stand.

Daddy reaches out to shake Bob Harper's hand. "Well, we really tried to get her to come back home, but she reminded me, 'a deal is a deal.' So, will you keep on taking care of Paula for me? I was afraid that after the newness wore off you'd be tired of having a house guest by now."

They smile at each other in understanding. Bob offers Pete a cigarette. While walking he confides to Pete, "Paula was sorely missed. She fits right in and there's no problem."

Pete retorts, "On the contrary, she would have returned with Father Maple had she thought of it."

Both men got a chuckle out of that.

Paula catches up with her dad and hugs him goodbye. Then she's off in the other direction in search of Annie.

The girls embrace each other. Annie wants to know all the details. Paula is quiet for a moment. She shakes her head and says, "Annie, in a million years, you just won't believe it."

"It's amazing how things can change in a week's time." Paula brings Annie up to date on all that happened during the week of her grandfather's funeral. She is too embarrassed to tell her everything her mother said to her.

The girls walk home alone for two nights. They have only gotten to talk about Paula's adventures and not caught up on all that has been happening at the lake.

At breakfast Paula asks, "What's been going on here? Breck and Chip didn't show up last night. That's two nights. Where are they?" Paula puts the bread in the toaster and cracks an egg.

Annie pours her cornflakes and takes the last of the milk. "I saw Breck yesterday morning around ten. He said he and his folks are going to Columbus to do some shopping while his dad tends to some railroad business. Chip went into Columbus with his sister, to visit their grandmother. ... I guess he goes in once a month. ... I think it's his mother's mother. ... Since Chip lives with his dad, that's the arrangement they worked out. I wish we'd get things worked out so I can see my mother." She pauses to rearrange the kitchen cupboard. "I think Daddy does have a girlfriend."

Paula chides Annie for not telling her last night. Annie apologizes saying that she was distracted by her dad's and Rusty's comings and goings. She notices some changes that arouse her curiosity but nothing worth discussing yet.

After breakfast Paula sorts her clothes so she can get some washing done. "When are the guys coming back?"

Annie removes the bobby pins from her hair. "Breck should be back tomorrow. I don't know about Chip. He just sort of disappeared."

"What's for dinner tonight?" Paula put the Rinso into the wash tub and swished it around to keep the powder from clumping.

Annie, while combing out her hair, says, "I haven't had a hair cut in six months. Daddy says I can get one when we go into Newark for groceries. Let's just eat at the park tonight. We're nearly out of everything."

Paula eats a second piece of peanut butter on toast while the clothes spin. After rinsing them and running them through the wringer she hangs them on the line that stretches across the back porch. "Let's try Oxydol instead of Rinso this time and we can't forget the green label, can we? ... We'd better get up to the stands. Anything going on I need to know about?"

Annie rinses the few dishes they used for breakfast and says, "I met a guy here last summer, Will Rolands. He shows up Sunday at the park. He has a friend with him. Bobby Nolan, I think his name is."

The girls grab their billfolds and head out the door.

"Will just stops by to say, 'Hi?' Do I get that right?" Paula gives a questioning glance.

Annie says, " No ... he wants more than that, of course. Seems his friend Bobby's dad just bought a new Chris-Craft ... a big one. Three seats and all that. Will wants to know if I have a girlfriend for Bobby. They want to take us out for a ride this week.  So, do I have a girlfriend?"

"What about Breck and Chip?" Paula considers.

"Yes, indeed. What about Breck and Chip? They've all but disappeared from the scene. I look at it this way. No one is going STEADY. No one is getting married. It's just a boat ride, for crying out loud."

Paula's thinking, *sure it's JUST a boat ride. It's JUST bowling a few games. It's JUST a movie.* These thoughts trip over themselves in her mind. "You don't even like boats, but it sounds like you really want to go. Are these guys special or something?"

The girls are close to the park entrance and Annie trips on some gravel and turns her ankle.

Paula catches her before she goes down. "Are you okay?"

"Yes, I think so." Annie turns her foot around a couple of times to be sure. "Will goes to North High in Columbus. Bobby goes to St. Charles."

That was the magic word even though the thoughts of a Chris Craft ride doesn't sit well with her. "The only guys I know at St. Charles are my two cousins and a guy from grade school who used to be my boyfriend. Hmmm! I don't suppose it would hurt anything to meet someone from St. Charles. In September I'll have to be thinking about someone to take to the fall dance. It isn't going to be Chip, now, is it?"

As they walk through the amusement park, people are opening their rides. The smell of stale beer from the 'Pinky' gives over to the smells of caramel corn and sugar waffles. The concessionaires wave hello as the girls pass. Mrs. Lax from the waffle stand says, "I missed seeing you. Where have you been?"

Paula is used to their caring ways by now. *Some just seem nosey. It is comforting to be missed. It makes me feel like I belong someplace.*

"Went to a family funeral." She calls as the girls pass. She turns to Annie and asks, "What's the plan?"

"Will said they'd come by this afternoon and meet you."

They reach the French fry stand. "I guess that's okay. Hi, Mister. Miss me?"

Rusty calls from the back, "Does a chicken have lips?"

Mister Harper scowls at Rusty's smart aleck remark. "Frankly, I did." He throws a load of potatoes into the tumbler. "I didn't realize what a good worker you are till I had Jessie sub for you. Fourth of July we were so busy we didn't have much training time to spend with her. It'll take the rest of the week to get the bookwork straightened out."

Paula knows what he means. Jessie is being factual while his books normally show a slightly different picture, she suspects. In other words, Mister doesn't want the park manager to notice any drastic changes that prompt questions for Mister to explain.

"I'm glad to be back. It's been a long week." Paula says while helping open the French fry stand.

"We've got one more big day coming up on the first Thursday in August. *Colored Day.*

"They'll be coming from far and wide. I hope there won't be any trouble. I smell change in the air." He keeps cutting potatoes. "They have the park for the whole day. The pool will be closed and no live music at the dance halls. I bought three extra bottles of lime syrup for the snow cones. The grown - ups seem to like their lime syrup. I bought an extra orange for the kids."

He continues, "Your dad said he tried to get you to stay with the family and not come back to the lake. I'm glad you chose to meet your obligation. I'm proud of you, Paula."

"I guess I'm growing up, huh?"

Annie raises her eyebrows and shrugs her shoulders in understanding. "Catch." She tosses Paula the money bag, five pounds of sugar and a bundle of paper for the cotton candy wands.

Paula, with full arms looks at Mister Harper and says, "I reminded Daddy we all made a deal and A DEAL IS A DEAL. So here I am." As she walks down the towpath she enjoys the musical strains of 'Nola' coming from the jukebox at the Pier Ballroom. "I'm home!"

# CHAPTER XIV
## SCORN

About three o'clock Annie comes down flanked by two guys. They are laughing and joking around. Paula likes the rapport Annie has with them.

Annie comes into the stand and scoops two snow cones. "What flavor, Will?"

"Grape with a drizzle of vodka," Will winks.

"Sure you do," as Bobby shoves him in the arm nearly knocking him over. "You'll give these fair lasses the wrong idea about us."

"Sorry! Skip the grape," Will frowns at Bobby.

"That's quite an introduction," Paula smiles at Bobby. "What is vodka anyway?"

"It's something his parents drink. Make mine cherry, Annie."

While Annie puts their money in the register, she says to Paula, "They want to take us for a boat ride about 6:30. I think I can get Dad to let us off," she adds softly, "Haven't heard a thing from Breck or Chip."

"You work it out. I'm game. Who is driving?"

Bobby raises his hand in the affirmative.

Permission was granted. The guys show up at 6:30 sharp. Rusty relieves Paula at the stand and the four of them head to Playland Pier. "Seems that's the best place to dock all boats short term." Bobby says.

Paula remarks to Annie, "He's more careful than Breck is with his dad's boat. Probably because it's new. Breck gets to drive more often."

Bobby carefully backs the boat away from the pier and eases out toward the middle of the lake. He guns the motor, then a sharp turn to the right toward Millersport. "Geez! That cherry snowball is talking." Annie squeals from the back seat. The jolt throws her into Will's arms. Every time Paula turns to say something to Annie she and Will are in a lip lock.

The driver, having accomplished his task for Will's sake, slows down the boat and puts his arm around Paula. "How do you like the boat?"

"It's peachy keen. Did your dad show you that maneuver?"

"Not really. He did experiment with quick and fast just to test its capabilities. Does it bother you?"

"I don't like experimental moves on this trip. I think it's best you do that on your own. We can't afford any mishaps. Right, Annie?"

Annie didn't hear a word Paula said.

"What year are you at St. Mary's?" Bobby asks.

"I'm a sophomore in September. What year are you?"

"I'm a junior. I'm on the basketball team. I'd like to play football, but I don't have what it takes."

"I go to the games. Maybe I'll see you there. Do you know John Mifflin?"

"Yes! How do you know him?"

"He went to St. Francis grade school until the eighth grade. Then his family moved to St. Stephan's parish. He finished grade school there. I hear he's quite popular. We called him 'Joker.' He always had a joke to tell about something."

"Cute! I don't know him that well."

"I was thinking about asking him to our Spring dance last May, but changed my mind and invited an Aquinas guy. My girlfriend asked John behind my back and since John knew Bernie, my date, we double-dated. We had a good time because the guys knew each other from St. Francis. I never trusted my girlfriend after that though. I don't really know a lot of guys from St. Charles."

"Well, you know one more now." Bobby nods and gives Paula a squeeze. He plants a kiss on Paula's cheek and turns the boat back toward the park. "Do you really like the boat?"

"Yes, I do." Paula is pleased with the evening. "It's really a nice boat. Tell your dad it's super," Paula says as she smoothed her skirt and composure.

"Uh! I don't think I'll tell him. I didn't exactly get permission to take anyone out but Will. I'll get permission though and we can go out again. OK?"

Bobby pulls up to the dock, kisses Paula full on the lips and then instructs Will to hop out and tie up. Will helps Annie out of the boat and the fellows walk the girls back to work.

Paula admits to herself: *I feel uncomfortable. I am missing Chip. I am hearing my mother's voice in my head. The concessionaires seem to be staring at us. Annie doesn't act like she cares very much.*

When Paula gets back to the snowball stand, Davie is there talking to Rusty. Davie stays after Rusty leaves.

"In for gossip?" he asks.

Paula gives him a questioning look. "I missed out on everything while I was gone, huh?"

"I'm talking today. How about lemon-lime," Davie waits for approval to talk.

Paula grinds the ice and scoops his cone. "So what gives?"

"Everybody who works up and down the towpath knows that Breck and his boyfriend haven't been around for a couple of days. Can I have some cotton when I finish my snow cone?"

Paula's interpretation is that he has something juicy to tell. She picks up a cotton candy wand and waves it slightly in Davie's direction. "And the rest of the story is …?"

"Everybody thinks Breck and Chip have two girlfriends because the four of them are seen together every night."

"Go on."

"The two girlfriends were seen with two new guys today. The new guys don't work at the park. No one knows who they are. Everybody is guessing that somebody is two timing our guys. What does 'two timing' mean?"

"It means it isn't nice to go out with somebody new when you already go with somebody else all the time."

Paula's feeling guilty as all get out when she tells him this. She's thinking not only about Bobby, but Slim from Perry County too. It's JUST a boat ride. It's JUST a movie. It's JUST bowling. Paula makes his cotton and he stays put.

"Anything else?" Paula gives him a look.

"Who are the guys? You ought to know by now the regulars don't mix with the vacation folks."

"Are you collecting information for the park folks? Are you their little spy? Are you on their payroll?"

"Reon did give me a quarter," Davie bows his head sheepishly as Paula questions his motives.

"And the quarter is supposed to buy information? Are you offering me the quarter?" Paula holds out her hand.

"I won't tell Reon if you don't want me to."

"You can spread the word that those two fellows are friends of Annie's from last year and Mister Harper knows the dad of one of them. They came over to the park to say "Hi," and show us the new boat his father bought. That's the whole story. Sorry it isn't any better than that. It's not a big deal. They're going back to Columbus soon."

"I gotta go. Thanks for the ice and cotton. I'll tell Reon the guys are old friends of Annie's."

"See ya later, little buddy." Paula waves.

Davie waves as he runs toward the High Striker.

* * *

Annie and Paula take their usual route home after closing. Paula says, "The folks watch us pass but turn their

152

heads away. They seem to be whispering after we pass their stands."

Mr. Calhoun, captain of the star boat line says, "Pretty fancy boat you took a ride in this evening."

Paula is sure her face turned beet red.

Annie says, "Yeah! Brand new. Dad knows his folks."

Mister Harper doesn't know him yet, but Annie will go back and clue her dad in. "He'll cover for us. He won't want any bad gossip about us because of the divorce," she assures Paula.

By the time they got back to the French fry stand, someone already told Mister Harper that Paula was a bad influence on Annie. The girls soon discover he already had to cover for them.

Paula acknowledges that her bad feelings about herself are piling up. *Leonard is twitching.*

Next day, Fr. Maple comes by. He and Paula talk a bit about the funeral and the unfortunate incident at the cemetery. When casual conversation is over, he says, "Some people around here are spreading unkind rumors about you. Anything you care to talk about?"

"Oh, no!" Paula tells him how the evening came about and her thoughts about St. Charles. Paula's eyes teared up. "I don't want to cause anyone any trouble. I don't like how I'm feeling."

*Leonard is restless.*

Father takes a Marlboro from his windbreaker pocket, lights it and flicks the match into the lake. "You see, honey, the folks who live out here pay attention to every movement. The park and village have a rhythm. When anything disturbs the rhythm, it's like a change in the weather. It gets talked about because there's so little going on in their private lives that they want anyone to know about. Any little thing gets magnified. It takes pressure off of them. I'll do my best to put a halt to any rumors. In the meantime, just go about your business and be your usual friendly self. I'll talk to Mr. Harper about being protective of your reputation. I wouldn't want any trumped up lies getting back to your folks. You never know who knows who from where out here."

When he mentions the possibility of Paula's parents hearing anything about her, all she can think of is the mean untrue accusations her mother made about her. Talk used to be about things and ideas. Now it seems to be about people and relationships. Life is being very complicated.

\* \* \*

Later that day, Chip comes around. "You don't waste any time replacing me, I hear."

"Oh no! Not you too." At this point Paula is mad. She throws a chunk of ice in the grinder. It makes a lot of noise but still doesn't drown out her thoughts.

"Are you going out with those guys again tonight or can Breck and I walk you home?"

She picks another chunk of ice loose and throws it in the grinder. She sticks the pick into the wooden post with energy she didn't know she had. "We won't be seeing them today." Paula is so emotional she can hardly talk.

She is glad to see Chip on the one hand, yet mad on the other hand. She is also afraid, embarrassed and ashamed. There is hardly room for all those feelings. *I guess that's what is meant by making a mountain out of a mole hill.*

*Leonard is shaking.*

Chip says, "If Breck had been here I'd have asked him to take care of you for me."

Jed's brother, Flip, an occasional Bozo walks by and calls out, "Do ya? Don't ya? Will ya? Won't ya?"

Paula, in near rage, says, "What the hell is that supposed to mean?"

*Leonard is hiding in the corner and crying.*

Paula is crying by now. She's thinking, *I can't even protect a lamb let alone myself.*

Through her angry sobs, she tries to talk. "I have had a really hard time since I've seen you. Maybe someone from the park has been talking to my mother. She is mean spirited and the people out here are being that way too. Nothing is how it appears to be."

Chip tries to put his arm around Paula but she pulls away.

He said, "I'm sorry I was not asking you about what happened instead of being smart and accusing you. Don't pay any attention to Flip. He's just plain crude. I am really sorry."

Paula wipes her eyes with a couple of paper towels and tries to compose herself. She is embarrassed that she had a melt - down in front of Chip. Everything is just being too much for her.

She wonders, *is this the end of a trust she thought she and Chip had? Was she two timing him like Davie said? Did she have a right to go with Annie? All these questions need sorting out. She just can't deal with them all at once in front of Chip.*

Breck and Chip pick up the girls like they did before they left town. They walk toward the Lake Breeze Hotel. Mitzi Joyce is playing and the room is packed. They go down the familiar steps to the parking lot. The mood is lighter by now. Chip has his arm around Paula.

Paula notices something in the gravel that looks kind of like a shriveled up white balloon. "What is that?"

When Chip sees it, he pulls her closer and puts his other hand over her eyes. "You don't need to know what that is." He pulls her aside then removes his hand from her eyes and kisses her. That kiss sends her spinning. She finally feels welcomed back. Paula seems to forget all about the object in question. Amazing, the power of a kiss!

155

Annie and Paula don't see Will or Bobby again. Eventually the buzz dies down among the concessionaires.

Breck, Chip, Annie and Paula happily go about their summer routine. Breck and Annie are exchanging kisses and holding hands now. Maybe the published boat ride woke up a couple of guys.

August 4, the first Thursday arrives. Paula is feeling a bit uneasy. She remembers the run-in with some colored kids while ice skating in Goodale Park in Columbus when she was nine. They acted like it was their park. There was some name calling. She asks Mr. Harper if Chip can help her in the stand. "I don't want to be alone if it's OK."

He agrees. "Good idea, Paula. I'll ask him officially if he'll be available to help you."

\* \* \*

The colored folks seem to be a happy lot tonight. They walk with an air of confidence. They dance around. They laugh and joke a lot. Everything is loud and funny. They are having a good time. They order a LOT of lemon-lime snow cones. About 9:00 in the evening Paula realizes why. As the laughter gets even louder a couple of guys start fussing over a bottle of something. As they buy the lime snow cones they add something to them from a bottle.

Chip says in a near whisper, "Vodka! That's why extra cops are on duty tonight."

A sort of argument breaks out between a guy and gal as they walk away. He is apologizing for eating somebody else's potato salad and not hers at the picnic. It didn't make any difference what he said. He wasn't going to win the argument.

Paula looks at Chip and just shrugs her shoulders. Soon everyone clears out leaving Paula and Chip alone.

They close the stand and enjoy a few quiet moments that make up for Paula's being gone for a week. *Leonard is not scared anymore.*

# CHAPTER XV
## YET ANOTHER INVITATION

It is the third week of August. Little by little the summer vacationers close down their cottages and take home the things for winter storage. There will be one final party for some. Labor Day weekend is the last hurrah. Tommy Dorsey is playing at the Pier Ballroom and the park will be teaming with young lovers while strains of 'Don't Sit under the Apple Tree' and 'Teach Me Tonight' fill the air. *Yes*, Paula thought, *So you say I've got a lot to learn. Teach me tonight.*

She and Chip are getting a little too cozy. She is afraid that sooner than later he'll try to 'teach me tonight.' She wants him to, yet feels afraid and guilty for spending so much time thinking about what there is to learn.

Annie and Paula start talking about school starting in September.

Annie is pin-curling her hair, which is quite long. She never did get the promised haircut. "Daddy is taking us in to see Mother this week. She's taking me shopping for school clothes."

"That's exciting. Are you going to get a new Maidenform bra?" Paula watches Annie looking at her profile in the mirror. "Remember how good the bras feel when they are new?"

Annie squeezes her bra and checks the straps and hooks. "I wonder what they put in that material that makes the cups so stiff. That's what makes them feel good. ... I think I might be ready for a 32B this time."

"Even if you are close, you can always use Kleenex to stuff. Better yet, ask your mother for a pair of falsies. I've got an idea. When we do our laundry tomorrow let's starch our bras. ... Heavily. ... Maybe that's what they do to new ones. Do you think anyone will smell the Satina?"

Annie swoons, "Woo, woo, woo! as she hurls a feather pillow at Paula."

They giggle and roll on the bed. Mister hollers his usual warning, "Pipe down up there."

Paula whispers, "You won't be wearing a uniform at Hebron High. Will you miss it?"

Annie is quick with, "'Is the Pope Episcopalian?' Go to sleep. We'll talk about starch in the morning."

After her daddy leaves next morning, Annie reaches under the kitchen sink and pulls out the laundry soap and holds up the Satina for Paula's approval. "Okay, Mad Chemist in the kitchen, get cookin'."

As ordered, Rusty pulled his dirty clothes from every corner of his bedroom and deposits them on the floor near the washing machine. Paula sorts colors while Annie washes the few breakfast dishes. Rusty leaves to catch up with his dad. The fun begins.

Paula joins Annie in the kitchen." Do you think I should triple the starch and half the water?"

With eyes big as half dollars, Annie says, "Maybe just doubling it for starters. I don't know how much time we'll have to correct the mistakes if it doesn't work. Just hang them on the line and let them drip dry enough to iron."

That afternoon, Paula's mother and dad show up. Mother reaches in her purse and pulls out an envelope addressed to Mr. and Mrs. Bradley from St. Mary of the Springs. Paula opens it.

The Dominican Sisters of St. Mary of the Springs Academy for Girls are pleased to invite Paula Bradley to attend her sophomore year beginning September 5, 1949. We look forward to her return.

Sincerely,
Sr. Mary Lauranna, O.P., Directress

Paula reads it out loud and smiles at her parents. "I guess that makes it official. I forgot that we are supposed to be invited back." She later learns that there are very few girls who don't receive an invitation to return.

Mother says, "We'd like to come back for you next week so we can do some shopping. You'll need a coat and a couple of outfits for the weekends. New blouses, tennis shoes and whatever else is on your list. You start the day after Labor day, so we can't wait until the last minute."

"Monday is my day off, but I'd like to have that time to say some goodbyes and be sure I have all my stuff gathered, if that's OK with you, Mother."

"We'll pick you up Wednesday then about 2:00 in the afternoon. Will that give you enough time?" she asks.

"That will be fine." Paula sighed. She was reluctant to think that everything is about to change and she's really not ready to face it. "Where is Jeniece?"

"She's playing with the kittens. She and the neighbor boy were dressing them in doll clothes and pushing them in the baby buggy when we left. His mother said she'd watch the pair this afternoon. We don't plan to stay long. I just wanted you to read the mail so we could plan our shopping date."

Daddy calls from the porch, "Are you ready, Mother?"

Mrs. Bradley hugs and kisses both the girls and says, "Next Wednesday at 2:00 then."

Pete and Bob finish their smoke and shake hands. Paula watches wistfully as the car heads toward Hebron Rd.

Annie rushes to the kitchen and sets up the ironing board to finish their experiment. The brassieres are damp dry. Perfect for ironing.

Paula very carefully irons dry every seam. When she finishes, the girls smile as the articles stand alone on the table. They can't wait to shower and try on their new idea.

\* \* \*

Off to work they go. Their project seems to be working fine. They experience that yummy new bra feeling they were striving for as they fill out their A cups.

Annie says, "I feel like everybody is looking at us."

"They are probably admiring our new profile," cajoles Paula.

The days are still quite hot. After about two hours working, Annie starts to itch and she is perspiring heavily. Paula is squirming also. She makes a trip to the French-fry stand to find out how Annie is doing. The French-fry stand is the warmer of the two. Paula works over the water and gets a breeze if there is one. She sees how miserable Annie is and asks Mister to send Annie home to change clothes. Paula offers to work the Corn Dogs if they can get Jessie to make snowballs. He agrees it's a good idea.

Paula advises Annie, "Soak your bra; wash the starch off of yourself; put my Johnson's baby powder on your red areas to calm you skin then let your bra drip dry again on the clothesline. Wear your bathing suit top under your blouse. When you get back to work, I'll take my turn. Sorry! I guess our experiment didn't work too well."

Mister is very observant but doesn't say much. He usually goes along with the girl's requests and they cooperate with his.

\* \* \*

Change is in the air. The nights are getting cooler. The next couple of days Chip helps Paula close. He cleans the cotton candy pan. There is hardly any business. Mister talks about closing the stand altogether when Paula leaves the lake. There is one cotton candy left in the holder. Who comes by but Davie?

162

"What's up, little buddy?"

"Is that cotton for me?" he asks, knowing there won't be many, if any more treats.

"It's got your name on it," Paula affirms.

Davie shares his latest information, "Reon's closing the High Striker after this weekend."

"Then what?" she prods.

How the park winds down for the season is all the buzz. Who is closing early? Where are they going? Do they plan to be back next year with the same players?

"We're getting a new trailer." Davie is quick to add. "Then we're moving to New something or other." He put some more cotton candy in his mouth. "I've been having toothaches. See? I lost one last night."

"You are growing up before my very eyes. Next summer you'll have a mouth full of new teeth."

Paula waves to him as he drifts up the towpath toward the fortune tellers. His sisters, Leah Rose and Donitza, are rarely seen in public. Paula has a warm place in her heart for them. She'll always be grateful for Leah Rose's advice. *So will Leonard.*

* * *

Captain Calhoun of the Star Boat Line is only driving on the weekends now. Everything seems to be gradually shutting down.

Paula counts the money and wipes down the snowball equipment. She ran out of cherry syrup last week. Mr. Harper says, "There isn't any point buying more. I still have a lot more lemon-lime left over from Colored Day."

The De Castro Sisters are singing, '... so you say I've got a lot to learn. Teach me tonight.' Paula tells Chip, "I'm going to miss Hank Williams singing, 'Got a feeling called

163

the blues, since my baby said goodbye,' and 'Heartaches.' Those songs will always remind me of this summer."

Chip says, "Yeah. It gets quiet quick around here when the music stops. ... A little spooky. ... We all are going to the Bus Station tonight. I have to see my mom."

"Sounds good. Is Breck still working?"

"No. Last night was his last night."

"What will you guys do then?"

"Get ready for school, I guess. There's a lot to do at home. The little ones all need new stuff. We'll be going in to Newark tomorrow." Chip takes care of the ice machine while Paula cleans the cotton candy pan.

Paula says, "Did I tell you my mother is picking me up next Wednesday at 2:00? We're going to Columbus to get my wardrobe ready for school. Even though I wear a uniform I still need weekend clothes. I also need to get my order in for a larger gym suit."

"How long will you be gone?" he asks.

"Probably shop on Thursday and return on Friday to work the holiday weekend." Paula tosses a wet towel at him which lands on his head.

There is little time left for the two of them to horse around. All is quiet for a while. Chip says, as he comes up behind Paula and kisses the back of her neck when no one is looking, "Looks like we'll be seeing less and less of each other. It'll feel like it did when you were gone for the funeral. I was lost every night from 9:30 to 10:30. Breck and I still walked Annie home but it wasn't the same without you."

Paula shivers and smiles. "I had no idea I was missed that much."

"Oh, yeah. Every time I saw Davie he asks, 'When is Paula coming back?' and I was reminded of how he always had a message for me from you." As he gave Paula another tender hug. "It's like the four of us have become a smaller family than with our parents, brothers and sisters. ... To think

164

that it's coming to an end soon makes me sad. Every year when the park closes it's like the end of a chapter and everyone is curious to see what direction the next chapter takes."

"Will you write to me or is the end of our chapter the end of our book?" Paula asks him.

"Ohhhh!" Chip groans. "I don't know if I'm any good at writing letters."

"If Annie isn't good at writing letters and you aren't good at writing letters, I won't know what's happening to any of you. Somebody has to let me know something. At least I need a picture of you to carry in my billfold." Paula urges as she pulls away from him.

"I'll promise you one letter by the end of September. Is that good enough?"

"Yes. I suppose we will all know by then how things are going for each of us. You are new at being a junior and I am new at being a sophomore. It's a little scary. What do you think will be the newest thing for you?" Paula risks letting her thoughts move to the next chapter.

Chip smiles, "Dad promises driving lessons."

"Oh, my gosh! Now that IS scary." They both laugh. "Will you come see me then?"

Chip queries, "Can we see if I pass the letter writing test first?"

"Of course. ... back up to NOW. ... Let's get the overhang down and locked so I can finish up and you can try out the last paragraph on me."

"As you wish, Miss." as Chip puts on some speed. "Time for some serious communication here."

They finish up the last of the chores. Chip lets down the awning and locks the corners. He comes back inside and wraps his arms around Paula They are aware that every kiss might be the last one.

The sky goes black. A huge clap of thunder sounds over Millersport way. Hank Williams fades, 'I've got a feeling' ... and then just the pelting of rain drops on the back and side of the snowball stand. No lights. No music. It's getting chilly on the outside but hot and steamy on the inside in more ways than one.

The storm ends much too soon. The juke box picks up where it left off. '… called the blues when my baby said goodbye. Got to thinkin' it over, all I did was sit and sigh…'

People emerged from their safe dry spaces. Activity at the amusement park resumes. "One more kiss before you leave me," Chip sings, imitating Sachmo. ... He says, "Give me a pencil and paper. I want to get your address and phone number. I'll be coming into Columbus to see my grandma. I hope I can see you then."

"Do you know when?"

"That's what I have to talk to my mom about."

Paula hugs him hard. She doesn't want to let go. They are getting closer as their time together grows shorter. They feel it but they had not talked about it. Tonight is different. Paula has no trouble talking about her feelings to Annie but was reluctant to learn if it was acceptable to share them with Chip. She is aware that a barrier has been breached now.

* * *

When Annie and Breck arrive at the closed snowball stand, Paula and Chip emerge. The four of them head to the Bus Station. "It's crowded tonight for some reason," Breck says. They wait for the big booth to be cleared.

Chip's mom motions them over. She doesn't say anything. She just brings the usual – lemonade for Chip, Pepsi for Breck, lemon Coke for Paula and an iced tea for Annie. She tosses bags of chips and pretzels on the table. "On the house tonight, kids."

166

She pulls a bottle of Horlich's malted milk tablets out of her apron pocket. "Here, Paula, I've been saving these for you."

Paula's eyes light up." However did you remember that I love them? Thank you so much."

More of the Lake kids arrive. J1 and J2 are with two new girls. Annie and Breck go to their table to meet them and find out what grade they will be in.

Chip's mother sees Chip and Paula alone finishing their drinks. She comes over to talk. "Chip will drive you into Columbus the weekend after Labor Day. You'll be staying at grandma's house, of course. You two go shopping for shoes and a winter coat. Don't come back without them. Paula, if you can join them Saturday evening, Sis can pick you up and take you home on Sunday morning in time for Mass. Would you like to do that?"

"I would love to. I know I'll miss everyone terribly. I'll check it out with my parents. I gave Chip my address and telephone number tonight so he can call me to find out if they say I can."

Annie and Breck return to our booth. They all thank Chip's mom for the drinks and chips. Most of the kids are gone now.

"Wait," Breck said. "Ma doo asked me to pick up Herbert Tarrytons for her." He and Annie leave for the cigarette counter.

Chip says, "I asked my mom if you could come to Grandma's and she said she'd have to work it out with Dad. I didn't know if she had done that until tonight. That's why I didn't say anything to you yet. Grandma has a little house in the country. You can sleep with sis and I'll get the sofa. I better tell you that Grandma doesn't have indoor plumbing."

Paula smiles and says, "I'm very familiar with outhouses and chamber pots. I can handle that. I look forward to it." She gives a quiet little laugh.

The four are together again and make the slow walk home in near silence. The crickets and tree frogs are so loud they could hardly hear each other anyway.

Since Mrs. Clark gave Mister permission to keep Annie and Rusty at the Lake, they will attend school in Hebron. Both are excited. Annie and Paula make plans to visit each other on holidays when Paula gets moved back to Columbus. Everyone has mixed feelings about saying "good-bye" to summer. J1 catches up with the four. He and Breck start singing , ". . .*with an engineer that's brave. Watch the curves that fill the tunnel. Never falter, never fail. Keep your hands upon the throttle and your eyes.*" they all chimed in, ". . .*Oh yes, your eyes.*" And they finished up, *"Upon the rail."*

"That's the truth," Paula says. ..."I'll always remember your blue plaid coat, Chip," she tells him.

"It's too small now. I tried it on this morning."

Eleven-thirty is approaching and the good night kisses are happening. J1 leaves them and heads toward his house.

Mr. Harper pulls in the driveway to drop off a sleepy Rusty. As was his habit, he calls out, "Good night, fellas," to Chip and Breck. He was indicating they should be leaving but they ignored his intention tonight.

Mr. Harper walks Rusty to his bedroom. They all said their good nights to him. Mister Harper adds, "I have some last minute business to take care of. You girls be okay with Rusty?"

"Sure. Don't be out too late," they beat him to his own advice.

Annie says as he leaves, "I think his last minute business has three daughters. I overheard a conversation between Mr. Jones and his brother about somebody named Helen – Mr. Jones said Helen was hauling Daddy's ashes. I've been trying to figure out what that means ever since I heard it."

The guys stifle a laugh.

Paula says, "How about a peanut butter sandwich?" She pulled the jar from the shelf. "There's a bucket of ashes in the shed that they probably are saving to use on the driveway in bad weather. Ice, snow, mud! ... "

Again the guys roll their eyes and Chip puts his hand over Breck's mouth.

"Could be. But why would somebody named Helen be hauling them?" Annie doesn't let go of the subject.

"Probably Helen of Troy. I don't know. Ask your dad." Paula answers.

"I'll ask Rusty. He spends more time with Dad than I do. I'll ask him if he knows anybody named Helen." Annie finds a jar with a little bit of grape jam left in it. "Want some?"

Paula shakes her head 'No.' So Annie put the jar back.

The guys didn't stay for sandwiches. Each kissed his girl goodnight with the usual plans to meet tomorrow.

* * *

Since the weather turns cooler at night now, the girls moved back upstairs for sleeping.

Annie said on her way up the steps, "'To bed, to bed,' said Sleepy Head."

"'Tarry awhile,' said Slow."

"'Put on the pot,' said Greedy Gut, 'We'll eat before we go.'"

Annie fights back the tears as she puts on her pajamas. "Mother used to say that at bedtime. I need to see her."

Paula turns out the light and crawls into bed.

Annie whispers, "Night."

Paula is feeling weepy about the memory of her conversation with Chip when closing tonight. However, the dark of night mixed with fog creeping in gives her a cozy feeling. It almost feels protective. August has always been a sad month for Paula. It was always vacation time for her

169

parents which meant a separation from them. Since her parents fought many times while drinking, Paula always felt like she was able to keep them from doing so. That feeling replayed every year without Paula's understanding why.

The girls sleep until the horse fly they'd been trying to swat breaks the morning silence. They get up and take turns using the bathroom.

It's about 2:00 Wednesday afternoon. The old blue Reo pulls up in front of the cottage. Mr. and Mrs. Bradley come to the door. "Anybody ready to go yet?" Paula's mother calls.

Hugs and kisses are exchanged. Bob Harper shakes Pete Bradley's hand as usual and off they go for a cigarette and man talk.

Mother says to Mr. Harper as he and Dad are leaving, "We've come to take Paula home, Mr. Harper."

He smiles and says, "It's been a pleasure to have her with us." He turns back to give Paula a hug good-bye. "When you get a break you're welcome for a visit anytime, Paula."

She wipes her eyes as she bids, "So long. Thanks for a wonderful summer."

Jeniece goes with Rusty and his cigar box out the back door.

Mister continues, "We'll all have busy days ahead. I'm taking the kids to see their mother on Tuesday. Then I'll have to close down the stands for winter. Then it's school clothes. I'll hardly have time to catch my breath." He doesn't mention anything about Helen.

Annie says to Paula, "I'll check the back porch, the bathroom and the front porch for hair brushes and stray socks while you pack your suitcase, okay?"

"Yeah!" Paula runs up the stairs. She is kind of ready but kind of not. With the last of her things put in the trunk of the car, she hugs Annie and says, "Remember, now, you promised to write to me. I want all the details. They'll be more important to me than to you probably."

"I will. I will. Good luck with shopping. Let me know what you get for the weekends and what color coat you get," Annie calls after the car while it's pulling away.

Paula says to her folks, "Mr. Harper didn't mind not having me work for Labor Day. We haven't been busy so a lot of the workers have closed their stands and some of the rides. I think there is going to be a Free Act though."

She asks Jeniece, "Where did you and Rusty go?"

Jeniece says, "Oh, he has three ugly toads he keeps in a box behind the garage. He wouldn't give me one though." She laughs. "He thought he'd make me scream when he showed them to me."

In tandem, both Mrs. Bradley and Paula say, "Thank God!"

Her dad just snickered and listened to the conversation,

Paula doesn't even think of Chip or Breck until they are on the road home.

Mother says, "Millie came over last night asking if you are coming back soon."

"Have you seen any of the other neighbor kids?

Dad piped up, "I saw one of your friends calling the usual command to her dog, 'Penny. *Geista heim, Penny!*'"

Paula smiles. "Do you think Penny's a rat terrier? Faster than the wind when she wants to chase a squirrel."

He says, "I wouldn't be surprised but I think she also has a little spitz in her."

Dad coughs and spits out the window. Paula ducks. Some things never change.

At last they are home. When she walks in the front door, it is like nothing has disrupted their lives at all. Daddy has his old job back. Paula has her bedroom back. Everything is the same as it was before Dad and Jeniece left for Junction City. Paula knelt down and kissed the floor.

171

The phone rings. "That sounds SO good, after a summer with NO phone. ... Millie wants to come over and help me unpack."

Jeniece joins Millie's brother do whatever it is they do. Paula sees them going toward Perry St. Jeniece is eight and going into third grade. That's how old Paula was when they moved back here from Richmond, Indiana.

Millie and Paula make plans to go to Lazarus.

Paula up-dates her who is mildly irritated that Paula hadn't written. "I need white uniform blouses, loafers and socks. I want Spalding saddles, but Mother says, 'Not till next month.' I've outgrown the ones from last year. Daddy slips me a $5.00 bill when Mother isn't looking."

\* \* \*

The first day of school finally arrives. Celia, Betsy and Lena beg, "Let's go to Lazarus to play records. Betsy's brother, Jerome, will be there with some St. Charles friends."

Paula is introduced to Jake Ward who promptly asks, "Can I have your phone number?"

Paula's rationale for going on the boat-ride with Bobby was because he goes to St. Charles and she didn't know anyone who did. Now, she does.

After an hour of records Celia purchases an album and they all board their respective busses. Jake and Paula soon discover they both take the W. Fifth Ave. bus. They continue getting acquainted. He knows my cousins. He asks, "Can you go to the movies this weekend?"

Chip is coming into town. Paula tells Jake "I'll be with a friend all night Saturday night."

Paula is thinking, *It's been two weeks already and not a letter yet from Chip. I know that he promised one by the end of September and I've been watching the mailbox every day. Nothing from Buckeye Lake at all. Communication is so hard without a phone. I've written him two letters already. I've been busy too.*

"OK if I call you to see when we can get together."

She shakes her head, "Yes" and gets off the bus with a wave. She sees the rest of the 'playground gang' in Coulter's drug store at the corner of Fifth and Perry. They don't even know she's been gone for the summer. She is being wrapped up by the neighborhood. It feels good to be back.

When Paula gets home there is a letter from Chip with his picture in it. "My sister will pick you up Saturday about 2:00. We'll go to a movie then to Grandma's house for supper. You and she will share the guest room. I get the couch. I'll take you back Sunday in time for Mass. Call me if this plan doesn't work for you."

She reads this part of the letter to Mother and Dad. "His Grandma lives on Denmarr Rd. in Linden. I don't know where it is."

Dad says, "I do. That's where Fred is looking to buy some land. It's barely out of town."

\* \* \*

Dear Diary, Sept. 1949,

I didn't read them the part about how busy Chip has been going into Newark four times for either something for the little brothers or himself. He's tired of it already. He said, "I really miss you. Since you aren't here all I want is more private time to remember our tender moments. We have an English teacher that stresses writing about feelings so I'll practice that with you if that's Okay."

Dear Diary,

    " Now I feel guilty about wanting to go to the
movies with Jake. Is life a series of these relationship
problems? "

    Leonard is shaking his head 'yes.' Later, PB


Dear Diary,

    I could think of nothing but the upcoming weekend.
Leonard has been very active. He doesn't seem to get too
excited about Jake who is really a convenience. Mother
encourages going steady so that there will always be
someone to date. I don't go along with that attitude really.
Seems easy and dishonest. I'll decide later after I think
about it some more.        PB


Dear Diary,

    The weekend was friendly as it could be with his sis
and grandma looking on. Chip did get to put his arm
around me in the movies. It took no time at all to connect
with our past feelings for one another but without the
daily exposure something was missing.  I'll have to think
about that too.

    His grandma's house has only a few lights. No inside
plumbing. I can't believe she still has an outhouse.
There's a pretty blue and white chamber pot under the
bed and I was given a flashlight in case I need to go
outside. I was not going outside in the dark by myself.

    After fried eggs and toast in the morning, Chip drove
me home. His temporary learner's permit requires that.
There are promises to write. More later... I think I feel
like I'm leading a double life. My parents don't have any
idea how close Chip and I became. They have no idea

about Blue Goose and the boathouse. They don't know about Fr. Maple, the summer storms and the nightly walks home. They only know me with the summer x'ed out. Their summer experience with me was not pleasant. They tried to make it pleasant but had no idea ... I'm in a quandry, Paula and Leonard.

Summer romances are difficult at best. The letters become fewer as Chip and Paula are immersed in their separate lives. They didn't get the nourishment required to nurture their relationship. They both have learning to do. *Leonard knows this but he waits for Paula to learn.*
Paula eventually agrees to go steady with Jake Wade. The very next day after she agrees to go steady, she gets a call from Bobby Nolan. The very Bobby Nolan who had his dad's new speedboat out and invited Annie and Paula to take one ride. *Yeah! Just one ride. Not a marriage proposal.* He turns out to be a classmate of Jake Wade. She has to refuse a date with him. ... if he had only called a day sooner ... But she's not the kind of girl that can go with three guys at the same time without having a nervous breakdown. Chip and Paula never discussed 'going steady.' They just went on with their lives. Whatever turned up, they dealt with it.

175

In early December Paula receives a letter from Annie.

"Dad bought the Dempsy house. We've been busy moving. I am now a cheerleader. That's why no communication. Chip's dad took a job in Tennessee or someplace that has mountains or something. I don't have any idea where Breck is moving. They still have the speedboat though so I assume it must be close enough to use it. I'm really sorry about not writing. I'll try to do better.

Love,
Annie

\* \* \*

In mid - December, Paula gets a call from Breck.
"Where are you calling from?" Paula asks.
"Here in Columbus. My family sold the house at the lake to Mr. Harper. We moved to the South End here in Columbus. I go to South High School now."
Paula is in shock. "What's going on at the lake?"
The lake is frozen. Ice boat races begin at the Yacht Club. ... Ice fishing for the hardy. ... J1's mother passed away. ... Annie's a cheer leader. She's dating somebody but I've lost track since so much is going on with our families. Mr. Harper married someone named Helen. Chip has his driver's license. ... Can you go to a movie with me this weekend?"
"I'm going steady." was Paula's blunt response.
"Well, it's just old friends getting together to talk about the Lake and what's going on."
Paula says, "Okay. Yeah! .I'll go Saturday night." She thinks ... *FRIENDS ... JUST ONE DATE* ... I don't have to see his dad ...

\* \* \*

Next day, she stands with Jake at the bus stop downtown where they each transfer to different busses to go to school.

Paula says to Jake, "A friend of mine from Buckeye Lake moved back to Columbus. We agreed to go to a movie Saturday night. He doesn't know anyone in town yet. I want filled in on our friends at the Lake so I hope you don't mind. He lives in the South End someplace."

Jake says, "I don't really like it, but I understand. Was he your boyfriend at the Lake?"

"No. He was my girlfriend's boyfriend. He's just new in town and I'm the only one he knows."

*Paula has a talk with Leonard. "Whew! I got over that bump in the road. All I have to do now is to get on the other side of the movies Saturday night ... then, ... get on with my life without further complications.*

*Leonard says, "heh, heh,heh. ... just a movie!"*

\* \* \*

Saturday night when Paula answers the door, she invites Breck in while she puts on her coat. "Good to see you. I was so surprised to get your phone-call." She introduces him to her parents.

Breck helps Paula with her coat saying, "You look nice. I've only seen you in summer uniform. You know! Shorts and jeans."

"I know. It feels good to wear real clothes again. Let's have a look at you. Maybe an inch taller ... summer crew cut grown out ... shaving, or am I allowed to notice that?" Paula asks.

"You have it all about right" He said while helping her into the car. "I just got my license. This is the maiden voyage of this boat and skipper, so to speak."

They both laughed at his comparison with the speedboat and the day they had of it with the lost necklace.

As Breck turns the car around at the dead end of the street he asks, "Where to?"

"Unless you've seen it, I chose 'The Third Man,' the new Orson Welles film. Or there's 'Adam's Rib' with Spencer Tracy and Katherine Hepburn which will be a romantic comedy. How do you feel about Orson Welles?"

"Welles it is. I'm not familiar with this end of town yet. Where to?"

Paula directs, "Turn left to Fifth Ave. and another left for about two or so miles. The Boulevard theater will be on your right, next to White Castle. Do you like sliders?"

Breck admits, "Don't know them yet."

"Well then, that's a must for later." Paula shakes her head.

After the film they grab a bag of eight and Cokes. The plan is to go back to Paula's. Everyone will be in bed so they can eat in the kitchen and talk. Paula wants all the details.

Breck starts talking. "The sliders are pretty good and the price is right. ... You know, Chip and I have been best friends for at least six years."

Shaking her head, Paula says, "I suspected that but I didn't know how long. ... Never thought to ask. So ..."

Breck takes a long draw from his Coke. "I knew my family planned on moving to Columbus. That isn't so bad. It's close enough to the Lake and we still have the Chris Craft. I know I'll be going back now and then. ... but when Chip tells me his dad's family is moving to Oak Ridge, Tennessee, I took it pretty hard. It's like a period at the end of our relationship."

Paula shares, "I've only gotten one letter from him since I returned to Columbus. It must have been before he knew he was moving."

Breck continues, "The job offer for his dad came up quickly and was accepted immediately. A defense job as I understand it. His dad had applications out to different places. Finally ... bingo!"

"Wow! ... My girlfriend's dad was kind of drafted to work for Curtis Wright during the war but I think his job ended shortly after the war was over. I never thought about continued Defense work. No reason to think about it, I guess. ... it feels like a cartoon. You know! Mickey Mouse tells Donald Duck some shocking news and Donald is knocked flat with surprise. It takes him a while to get up after he deals with the news."

While trying to absorb her personal implication, Paula sits quietly ... within herself.

*Leonard has been through the exercise before so he waits for all the information to sink in.*

Breck interrupts her pensive moment, he said. "Chip asked me, 'Do me a favor, will ya?... While I'm gone, ... take care of Paula for me.'"

Paula didn't hear Leonard say, ... ***"Uh Oh!"***

THE END

## Epilogue

The sophomore year had its chills and thrills. Breck follows Chip's instructions to take care of Paula.

*Yes, life IS like a mountain railroad*
*With an engineer that's brave.*
*You must make the run successful.*
*From the cradle to the grave.*
*Watch the turns that fill the tunnel.*
*Never falter, never fail.*
*Keep your hands upon the throttle*
*And your eyes. - - Oh yes, your eyes- -*
*Upon the rail. . . "*

Should the reader or anyone known to the reader who suffers from the victimization portrayed in this story, be it female or male, know that help was not available psychologically, legally or physically in 1949. Today is a different story. There are laws and counselors with special skills available for those who are willing to ask for the help that IS available.

Memories don't just go away. They fester and show up in unrelated areas that sabotage the victim. It can manifest as irrational fear, anger, cruelty to those you love, night tremors, bed wetting, and so on. Parents especially be advised that instruction to watch your child's behavior is not enough. Know what you are looking for and act on it. Children don't know how to talk about sexual abuse. It is up to the parent, teacher or baby sitter to be observant and act on your suspicion and/or knowledge. Let a professional make the final evaluation.

The victims surely need help. The perpetrators and families need help as well. Even if the deed was done long ago, the memory of unprocessed pain can accompany you to the grave needlessly. It is never too late. Your reaching out for help might surprise you. You could be giving courage to other family members who were victims also. You may be validating their experience.

I'd like to be able to say, "Get help from your minister or priest." However, they are not the ones with the skills mentioned above. Anyone who asks you, "not to tell," is not the one who will help you. You must "tell" the right people to get the help needed. This is the courageous thing to do. No one says it is easy. Just shut your eyes, grit, your teeth and do it. Peace of your mind and safety of your body makes up the you that you are. You are important. You are entitled. There IS someone out there who can and will help you. Pray for guidance and the strength to follow through.

## RESOURCES

State **Resources [RAINN] Rape,** Abuse and **Incest** National Network
www.rainn.org/ Get Info or Get help
State Resources From anywhere in the U.S. Call the **National Sexual Assault Hotline** 1-800-656-HOPE(4673) or call202-433-3064 to reach the RAINN ...

**International Sexual Assault Resources [RAINN] Get Help**
Rape crisis centers outside the U.S. Are not associated with RAINN.
RAINN is searchable by county, plus index of domestic violence resources in over 70 languages.
Google resources for rape and incest counseling for more information.

Patte Burgoon was born in Columbus, Ohio not far from the ancestral farm in Perry County. A year out of high school she married, migrated to Cleveland and then to Detroit area where she single parented seven children while teaching piano at Detroit Institute of Musical Arts. Her divorce and remarriage took her to the Pacific NW where she became a trained rape and incest counselor.

Patte had been a member of Michigan Music Teachers Association and National Guild of Piano Teachers but hearing loss forced her to forsake the piano. Following two years in Seattle she moved to San Diego, California where she enrolled at Mesa Community College, then on to San Diego State University to earn a master's degree in rehabilitation counseling. She joined a rehabilitation firm in New Mexico where she worked as a counselor for injured workers. Her husband remained in California. Patte was unable to maintain a long distance marriage so she returned to Columbus, Ohio where she retired.

She always felt she would write a book about Buckeye Lake, Ohio. It was now time to hone her writing skills by joining a writing group. She attended classes on memoir writing, retraced old familiar territory and was now encouraged to write her book. She won a prize in a national contest while in college writing about hearing loss. She entered two juried poems and three short humor based pieces and is published in an anthology: *Works in Process: Women Over 50 Reflecting.*

*Buckeye Lake Summer1949: Take Care of Paula for Me* is a novel based on experiences of the main character, Paula Bradley who lives the summer with a newly divorced man, his 14 year old daughter, Annie, who is Paula's best friend and Annie's ten year old brother, Rusty. The book can be viewed as a story of first love, a coming of age piece, and one depicting hard decisions families make when life demands it. It is based on people she's known and loved. Patte follows the words of an old Appalachian hymn, *Life is Like a Mountain Railroad.* Many parts of the book seemed to write itself like in the use of the hymn, portrays such as the crisis, and the return to Paula's normal life all giving a sense of how it was to deal with time and space in 1949 without modern technology.

Patte shows the reader a vital summer community that came alive from Easter Sunday to Labor Day in years past. The deck has been shuffled and embellished to show what life was like for a young teen working at the amusement park, then called 'Playground of Ohio' in 1949. She invites you to enjoy a bit of the pain Paula endures and sweetness that made the summer bareable.